Not free, Sian was furious

It was Nick's damned rule about mixing business with pleasure, not hers!

"It may come as a shock to you," she snapped, "but I have no wish to feature in your life! That's the sort of thing you should try telling that battalion of women constantly ringing you here. I'd have some peace then to get on with my work."

"Do they bother you, Sian?" he asked mockingly, slowly advancing on her. "Because they don't bother me." His hand streaked out and caught her wrist as she turned to make her escape.

"You're the only one who bothers me," Nick murmured, tugging her against him. "And you're a hypocrite if you refuse to admit the feeling is mutual."

KATE PROCTOR is a British writer who has lived most of her adult life abroad. Now divorced, she lives with her two grown-up daughters and her cat Wellington. She is a qualified French teacher, but at present devotes all her time to writing.

Books by Kate Proctor

HARLEQUIN PRESENTS

Don't miss any of our special offers. Write to us at the following address for information on our newest releases.

Harlequin Reader Service
901 Fuhrmann Blvd., P.O. Box 1397, Buffalo, NY 14240
Canadian address: P.O. Box 603,
Fort Erie, Ont. L2A 5X3

KATE PROCTOR

reckless heart

Harlequin Books

TORONTO • NEW YORK • LONDON
AMSTERDAM • PARIS • SYDNEY • HAMBURG
STOCKHOLM • ATHENS • TOKYO • MILAN

Harlequin Presents first edition August 1990
ISBN 0-373-11292-0

Original hardcover edition published in 1989
by Mills & Boon Limited

CHAPTER ONE

'WHY on earth have they the idea that Nicholas Sinclair's some sort of ogre? It's ridiculous!'

Sian McAllister glanced up from the pad on which she had been doodling, interest enlivening the delicate beauty of her features. The plump, rather motherly woman who had spoken sounded agitated.

Sian's wide-spaced, blue eyes scanned the huge rectangular table of the conference-room. Poor Margaret, she thought, with a twinge of unease—barely half the staff had bothered to put in an appearance. Her eyes rose pleadingly to those of Anna Walker, the attractive, dark-haired girl seated opposite her.

'Margaret, I'm sure no one thinks that,' murmured Anna, her placating tone lacking much conviction. 'The meeting was called at rather short notice. If you like, I'll see if I can round up——' She broke off, relief creeping over her face as the door behind Sian opened and three men burst in.

'Sorry, Margaret,' apologised Alan Hunter, a burly, handsome man in his fifties. 'But at such short notice, I'm afraid this is as many of us as you'll find available.' He glanced round the half-empty table as he took a seat next to Anna.

Sian was mentally trying to pin-point Alan Hunter's role in Sinclair Lawson Publishing—even after eight months with the company she still found the odd name and title eluding her.

'How did the trip to New York go, Mags?' asked the second of the late-comers, winking conspiratorially at

Sian as he lowered his long, lanky frame into the seat next to hers.

Bill Gardiner she had no difficulty in placing, noted Sian, grinning back. He was head of the historical section—and the only one in the company who actually called Margaret Fell 'Mags' to her face.

'That's what I've been hoping to get around to,' sighed Margaret, for once dispensing with pointing out how she loathed that contraction of her name. 'I was just saying to the others—I honestly don't understand why everyone seems to have the idea Nicholas Sinclair is some sort of ogre,' she repeated anxiously.

'I don't know about ogre,' chuckled the third of the men, taking a seat, Sian was relieved to see, at the far end of the large table. 'But judging from some rather interesting rumours I've been hearing, the girls will need to be on their toes.'

Sian felt her blood begin to boil—coming from him, that was ripe! She was pleased to see the positively withering look to which Margaret was now treating him.

'I should have thought his being the sole proprietor of the company which happens to employ you would have been of more interest to you than any rumours concerning his sex appeal,' pointed out Margaret Fell sharply.

'Do I take it we're about to get down to the nitty-gritty of this meeting, Margaret?' asked Alan Hunter quietly, his eyes shrewdly watchful as they held the woman's.

'I was merely pointing out that Peter Lloyd's remark was somewhat sexist—but then, most of Peter's remarks are,' replied Margaret.

'But it makes a change for a man to be on the receiving end of them,' muttered Anna Walker, flashing the man a contemptuous look.

'For heaven's sake!' exploded Margaret, as Peter Lloyd sarcastically blew the enraged Anna a kiss. 'Could we get on with the reason for this meeting? As you all know, I've been in New York for the past few days—with Mr Sinclair.' Every eye in the room became trained on her. 'And, as you also all know, Sinclair Lawson has been more or less limping along pretty much under its own steam since Wally Lawson died three months ago.'

'I'm not sure that I go for limping,' protested Alan Hunter. 'I agree Wally always had his finger on the main pulse, and that we're all missing him like hell . . . but it's Wally as a person we miss.'

Every person in the room nodded.

'Margaret, even *you* have to admit it was Wally's penchant for delegating that kept Sinclair Lawson what it is——'

'Yes,' interrupted Margaret quietly. 'And he kept it as what many would regard an anachronism. In no way could Wally ever be described as a go-getting American businessman. He was an out and out Anglophile who not only revelled in, but positively encouraged, Sinclair Lawson's reputation of being eccentric.'

'OK—so we're the eccentrics of publishing,' agreed Bill Gardiner. 'But we're also profitable.'

'Profitable—but by what yardstick?' asked Margaret.

'So that's it,' sighed Alan Hunter resignedly. 'Our new American proprietor is only interested in the bucks.'

'We've *always* had an American proprietor,' retorted Margaret sharply. 'It was Sinclair money that bought out Goodman's, which, for those of you unfamiliar with the history of this company, was its original name. All right, it was Wally's free hand that maintained the unique—yes, eccentric—Goodman reputation. But the money behind all this was never Wally's, which is why, on his death . . .'

Both Sian and Anna leapt to their feet in consternation as Margaret showed every sign of breaking down. They sat down again as the older woman managed to get a grip on herself.

'Which is why the company has now reverted to the control of Nicholas Sinclair.'

'Margaret, we all loved Wally,' stated Bill Gardiner contritely. 'And I suppose we've all just got to face up to reality. So tell us—what's young Sinclair like?'

'I like him very much,' replied Margaret, now completely in control of herself. 'I'd say he's a very open and fair-minded young man. He's interested in the company and wants to know what makes it tick. And as for being interested only in bucks,' she added, flashing Alan Hunter a rebuking look, 'the Sinclair family is numbered among America's wealthiest. If they wanted more, they'd hardly be looking to a relatively small, London publishing company to find it.'

Alan Hunter managed to look suitably contrite. But he hadn't finished. 'So what possible interest can a successful New York lawyer—I've done a bit of homework—of considerable personal wealth, have in this company?' He sounded genuinely puzzled.

'Search me,' muttered Bill Gardiner, then added, with a humourless laugh, 'though his law background could come in handy with the likelihood of a hefty lawsuit hanging over us. Hell, as things stand, if Joel Henderson goes ahead the case is bound to go against us and we can forget all about profitability!'

Margaret Fell gave a small shudder, but chose to ignore Bill's words.

'All I know is that the father and Wally had an agreement,' she stated. 'Whereby Sinclair Lawson passed to Nicholas Sinclair on Wally's death—and that Nicholas Sinclair has decided to move to London . . .'

'And step into Wally's shoes?' asked Anna.

'If he decides that's what he wants—yes,' agreed Margaret. 'He's coming tomorrow. I'd just like to see him given a fair chance—not have him confronted by what virtually amounts to hostility.'

'Margaret's right!' exclaimed Sian, impatience in the eyes that took in the mainly glum faces around the table.

'And how would you know, gorgeous? You've hardly been with the company five minutes,' drawled Peter Lloyd.

Sian flashed him a look of utter contempt. 'I'd have thought you of all people would have known it's eight months—or perhaps time just flies when you're wasting your breath on your chatting-up routine. Mind you, five minutes was all it took me to discover you were the resident lech!'

The tall, sandy-haired man, who had managed to reduce her to almost gibbering rage on her first day, still blatantly propositioned her whenever an opportunity arose—only now she had learned to do as the rest of her female colleagues —she cut him dead.

'Perhaps Sinclair won't find you quite so uncooperative. I hear his problem is more one of fighting off the girls.'

'And won't that put your nose out of joint!' snapped Sian, in the heat of the moment forgetting her vow never to give him the satisfaction of a reaction. 'Just imagine—he could fire all the opposition and take his pick of the women . . . didn't they have a saying about American men years ago—over-paid, over-sexed and over here?'

'Sian,' groaned Anna, her eyes flashing pleading signals

across the table.

'No! Why shouldn't I say what I think?' exploded Sian. She was sick and tired of the likes of Peter Lloyd—only the other day he had reduced a temporary clerk to tears.

'Why not, indeed?' remarked a quiet voice from immediately behind her.

Sian started, her eyes moving from Anna's frantic gaze to Margaret, whose face was now scarlet with embarrassment. The voice that had spoken from behind her had been deep, almost musical—but what now struck her most forcefully was that it had contained an accent that was unmistakably American.

'Mr Sinclair—we weren't expecting you until tomorrow,' stammered Margaret, rising to her feet.

Sian felt her shoulders sag, a silent groan of disbelief echoing hollowly inside her, while her eyes flashed messages of murderous intent at the grinning face of the instigator of her outburst.

Nerve-rackingly conscious of the movements to her left, her eyes dropped to the polished wood table-top, then moved towards the figure beside her, now almost in her line of vision.

'I decided to call in today. I have something you might find of interest . . . but we can discuss that later,' the man was saying.

Sian's eyes were now travelling slowly up the pale, lightweight raincoat on the figure beside her, travelling slowly because they dreaded coming to the face and what they would find there.

What exactly had she said? Hell—her mind was refusing to co-operate, she realised in panic, as Margaret's words, followed by more with that distinctively attractive, musical quality, drifted around her ears.

Suddenly she was wishing her mind had stayed an uncooperative blank, as her earlier words rampaged back into her awareness.

By now her eyes had reached broad shoulders, and were moving upwards with an almost fatalistic compulsion. He was either very tall, or the painstaking progress of her eyes was making him appear so, she told herself, as her fixed gaze reached the gleam of thick, dark mahogany hair, the tawny streaks of gold glinting in it seeming to indicate time spent in constant sunshine.

Her eyes flitted towards the profile, then darted back to the safety of the hair. The fact that he was younger than she had imagined, probably in his early thirties, and that the profile she had glimpsed had shown strong, even features, was neither here nor there, she reminded herself miserably, as Margaret continued introducing him to those present.

Soon they would get round to her, she realised, with a stab of total panic. For heaven's sake, she told herself sharply, the man was bound to realise he had heard her words out of context . . . wasn't he?

'And, lastly, we have the newest member of our team—Sian. Sian McAllister. She's been with us only eight months, but it was Sian who discovered Lucy Walton for us,' said Margaret kindly, obviously feeling the need to put in a good word for the visibly squirming Sian.

'Hello,' murmured Sian uncomfortably, wondering if she should shake hands—she was the only one near enough to be able to do so.

Knowing what an idiot she must look, with her gaze now seemingly riveted on the table-top, Sian's eyes rose to those of the man now looking down at her.

He *was* tall. And he had quite extraordinarily beautiful

eyes—once one had got over the shock of the startling coldness of their blue. Any thoughts she may have had about offering him her hand were quickly dispelled as his head dropped a fraction in what could only be termed as a dismissive nod.

'I think the best way for us to get acquainted is for me to meet each member of staff individually.' It was the deceptive softness in his voice that made his statement seem more of a suggestion. 'I'll try to cause as little disruption as possible to routines, but we'll start the meetings first thing tomorrow. Margaret will let you know when I'll see you.' Though that soft accent still imparted its illusion of gentleness, there could be no mistaking that an order had just been issued.

He turned to Margaret, still standing beside him. 'Perhaps, when you've finished here, you could show me an office I could use?' he murmured, with a smile as unexpected as it was quite stunningly appealing.

'I've finished here,' Margaret assured him, her answering smile erasing any lingering anxiety from her features as she followed him from the room.

'Well done, gorgeous,' murmured Peter Lloyd, breaking the almost stunned silence that had descended on the room.

'Give it a rest, Lloyd,' snapped Alan Hunter. 'It's thanks mainly to you our new employer probably thinks he's got himself saddled with a bunch of virulent anti-Americans.' His gaze moved to Sian, his expression one of pained disbelief. 'Perhaps, in future, you'll think twice before letting rip like that.'

'She could hardly have known the man was going to walk in like that!' exclaimed Anna indignantly. 'And besides, just about every female on the premises has complained about Peter's behaviour at one time or another. The only one of you men who ever listens to us with anything approaching sympathy is poor Simon——'

'*Was* poor Simon,' cut in Bill Gardiner. 'We'll deal with Peter and his wandering hands another time. Right now, we ought to consider the question of Simon. As things stand, the whole Joel Henderson mess is down to him—and the repercussions could be catastrophic for his financial future.'

Every face around the table became uniformly glum.

'Wally always stood by his team, no matter what,' stated Alan Hunter quietly. 'But we're no longer dealing with Wally.' He hesitated. 'Hell, you might as well know now as later—Simon's stroke has put paid to his ever working again.'

'But Mrs Porter told me most of the paralysis has gone!' exclaimed Sian, shaking her head in protest.

It had been as Simon Porter's assistant that she had been taken on by Sinclair Lawson. Every scrap of knowledge she had acquired of her job—every ounce of the self-confidence slowly built up in her—had come courtesy of that genial, endlessly patient, lovable, bald-headed bear of a man. The severe stroke Simon Porter had suffered less than a month ago had affected her far more deeply than Wally Lawson's earlier death.

'Love, I know what his wife's been telling you. But Margaret and I actually saw him just before she took off for New York,' Alan told her gently, then shook his head grimly. 'I'm afraid his career is definitely over . . . hell, the man's only fifty-five!' he exclaimed bitterly.

Simon's age came as a surprise to Sian. To her he seemed almost the archetypal, absent-minded professor—a man who had somehow struck her as being at least ten years older than his actual age.

'As I was saying,' continued Alan Hunter, 'Wally would have seen him all right, despite this possible lawsuit hanging over us. But, without wishing to sound alarmist, I'd say Sinclair would be well within his rights to fire him—if things are as they appear.' He slammed his hand impatiently on the table as a burble of protest broke out around him. 'Hell, I can't believe it any more than you can! But everything points to Simon having completely ignored all the legal aspects involved—as though the laws of libel were an alien concept all of a sudden——'

'All of a sudden!' exclaimed Bill Gardiner. 'Alan, no man of Simon's calibre would suddenly behave so completely out of character! No matter how unorthodox his methods, he was a stickler for the rules. If he chose not to consult Sinclair Lawson's lawyers, it can only be because he had watertight proof of the material.'

Alan Hunter shrugged helplessly. 'I agree, but Margaret and I have been through every paper we can lay hands on—not that Simon believed much in filing systems. You know what he was like, he kept most things lying in a pile on his desk-top! And Margaret's grilled Sian, though she could hardly be able to shed much light on the subject —the whole thing had been more or less sewn up by the time she came here.' Despite his words, his eyes turned almost pleadingly to Sian.

'I've been racking my brain for weeks now,' she sighed. 'I've even managed to compile a couple of files on it . . .' Her words petered to a despairing halt.

'Despite all the evidence to the contrary, no one who knows him would find it easy to believe that Simon could have been so uncharacteristically negligent,' sighed Alan. 'But nothing can alter the way things appear right now . . . which brings me to our meetings with Sinclair tomorrow.'

All faces were turned expectantly towards him.

'Obviously, none of us is going to raise the subject. But if Sinclair happens to . . . we'll just have to play our cards as carefully as we can to stall him—plead ignorance to the whole background of the case, if necessary.'

'Could I say something?' asked Sian quietly. 'After the way I blotted my copybook today, I wouldn't be in the least surprised if my interview consisted of "you're fired".' Her eyes met those of Peter Lloyd who, for once, had the grace to look a little sheepish as he echoed the protests of the others. 'As I was working for Simon, I could say he left me to deal with the legal aspects . . .'

'Simon never would have,' sighed Bill.

'But Mr Sinclair wouldn't know that!' exclaimed Sian impatiently. 'Look, if he's going to fire me, what the heck!'

'I doubt if the man's likely to be that small-minded,' murmured Bill, adding with a chuckle, 'though, taken out of context, your words were hardly endearing.'

'If he's not the type to fire me for that, there's hope he might make allowances for my complete ignorance of publishing procedures. If Simon's fired, he could lose everything—probably most of his pension rights, and you know Wally would have given him the full whack, if not more!'

A silence fell round the table as Sian finished speaking, and she found herself having to stifle a sudden twinge of wry bitterness as she imagined their reasoning. She could hardly blame them for probably seeing her as not being in need of the income she in fact needed desperately. For a start there was the exclusive area many of them knew she lived in; then there was the unmistakable quality of her clothing and accessories—though probably only the women, and few of them, would have been aware that the majority of her outfits carried the labels of some of the most exclusive of couturier houses in Europe.

'Sian, it's very sweet of you,' said Anna gently.

'It is,' agreed Bill. 'And heaven knows, it might even come to taking you up on it. But for the time being we'll just have to play dumb and hope something turns up to vindicate Simon.'

As Bill spoke, Sian was deep in thought. Something niggling at the back of her mind suddenly came to the fore.

'Alan, you've seen Simon,' she stated quietly, apprehension creeping into her eyes. 'Why didn't you just come out and ask him?'

There was a flash of anguish in Alan Hunter's eyes before they dropped beneath the probing gaze of Sian's.

'Because . . . paralysis has made speech difficult.' The knuckles of the fingers linked together on the table before him whitened as they suddenly clenched fiercely. 'It's pointless pussyfooting around,' he declared unhappily. 'It's made speech impossible. Not that speech would help—very little is registering with Simon at the moment, though his doctors are hopeful this is only temporary.'

'Poor Mrs Porter,' sighed Sian. 'She always tries to paint such a bright picture whenever I ring.'

There were so many questions she wanted to ask, but she found herself biting back the words. The deep affection that had grown between her and the stricken man made her wish she had never asked the original question which had brought such a heart-breaking reply.

'Your turn,' announced Anna Walker, smiling encouragingly as she approached her own desk which—since

Nicholas Sinclair had chosen to use the office adjoining
hers for his interviews—Sian had appropriated for almost
the entire day. 'And stop looking as if you're about to face a
firing squad,' soothed Anna. 'He's utterly charming—and
no mention of lawsuits.'

Sian rose, feeling exactly as she imagined someone facing
a firing squad would. The fact that he had chosen Simon's
office instead of Wally's had unnerved her for some
indefinable reason. As had also the fact that each inter-
viewee had emerged virtually singing Nicholas Sinclair's
praises—Alan and Bill had come out looking positively
hopeful.

All this should have given her hope, she told herself as
she made her way through her own office and knocked on
the heavy oak door leading from it. But it hadn't. The only
comfort she had found had been in hearing, time after time,
that Joel Henderson's name, and the possibility of a lawsuit,
had not been mentioned.

'Come in.'

Sian took a breath that threatened to overload her lungs,
then opened the door.

There was a half-smile on the face of the man who rose
politely as she entered. It remained on that almost
aggressively handsome face as Sian took the seat before the
large, rectangular desk, which she still regarded as Simon's,
and it was a smile she found frankly unnerving, containing
as it did neither warmth nor welcome.

'Miss McAllister—Sian,' he murmured, his eyes on an
open folder before him as he returned to his seat. 'Is that a
Scottish name—Sian?' he asked.

'No, Welsh,' replied Sian, feeling less at ease now than
she had ever done in her entire twenty-three years. 'The
McAllister's Scottish, though—I suppose I'm a bit of a

mongrel.' What had possessed her to come out with an inanity like that? she groaned inwardly, as those incredibly cool eyes flickered from her file to her face, then back to the file.

'Which would you rather answer to—the Welsh or the Scottish?' he enquired evenly.

Sian looked at him blankly, wondering if he could actually be asking her to state a preference for a particular nationality.

'Sian, or Miss McAllister—which would you prefer me to call you?' he explained, the merest hint of impatience creeping into the softness of his words.

'Oh—Sian!' she exclaimed, relieved.

'I answer to Nicholas, Nick, and sundry other variations . . . in fact, to anything within the bounds of reason.'

Sian's head ducked slightly—a purely reflex reaction of escape from what seemed the sharp message in those coolly uttered words.

She might as well get it over with, she urged herself, her hand reaching up to flick aside the heavy curtain of dark blonde hair now falling irritatingly across her face.

'Look . . . I realise I owe you an explanation for what you overheard yesterday,' she blurted out.

'Having already listened to several rather confusingly vague variations on that particular theme today, I'd rather give yet another a miss, if you don't mind.'

Sian's eyes widened noticeably. She had prepared herself for having difficulty in explaining her remarks—but not for being given no opportunity whatsoever to offer an explanation.

'If that's the way you want it,' muttered Sian uncomfortably.

'That's the way I want it.'

Something in his tone brought Sian's eyes to his face, just in time to catch the tail-end of a slight quirking at the corners of his mouth. It was a mouth she might well, in different circumstances, have described as generous in its strong definition. But now she saw only its harsh edge of cruelty, and knew with a certainty that chilled her that this was a man few would cross without paying a heavy price.

'So . . . tell me, Sian, what's your particular role in Sinclair Lawson?'

'I've become a sort of general dogsbody since Simon had his stroke. Simon Porter, I mean. I was engaged as his assistant, dealing mainly with unsolicited manuscripts.'

'Among which you found Lucy Walton.'

'Anyone would have noticed her—anyone who likes children's stories. They seem to be hoping she'll be the new Enid Blyton.'

'And we'll have you to thank if she is.'

Alerted once again by that indefinable something in his tone, Sian glanced up suspiciously. The blue eyes regarding her from across the desk contained the unmistakable gleam of mockery. As she felt the colour rise in her cheeks, her chin lifted in defiance.

'Don't you think it would be best if you let me explain what I was saying yesterday?' she demanded, throwing caution to the winds.

'Why?' he asked, his tone now openly mocking.

'Because I don't happen to be a particularly paranoid person, yet I get the distinct impression you intend this interview to be nothing more than a joke at my expense!'

'And you call that being not particularly paranoid?' he asked with exaggerated amazement, tilting his lean, broad-shouldered body back in the swivel-chair with the air of one thoroughly enjoying himself.

'If you're hoping I'll lose my temper—giving you an excuse to fire me with impunity—no doubt you'll succeed!' Sian exclaimed, her temper snapping as she leapt to her feet. 'A more honest man wouldn't have stooped to such a ploy—he'd have fired me when I first walked in!' With an angry toss of her head, she turned and made for the door.

Before she could reach it, he was in front of her, his bulk effectively barring her way.

'Wow! I always considered I had a short fuse,' he murmured, a gleam of what was suspiciously like admiration warming the coolness of his eyes as they flickered across the creamy oval of her tense, angry face.

'Would you mind getting out of my way?' she demanded, disconcerted to find her sudden burst of fury rapidly dwindling.

'Sian, if we're to be a team, I think it might be an idea to lay down a few ground rules if blood isn't to be spilled.'

'Would you mind speaking English? I didn't understand a word of that,' snapped Sian, only to find the impetus of anger deserting her completely with the sudden transformation of the face gazing down into hers.

The lazy smile curving the corners of his mouth was no incentive to maintaining anger. It was a smile that transformed the almost classical proportions of his features from cold aloofness to decidedly engaging appeal.

'You know, if I weren't such a thick-skinned person, I might almost have taken that remark as anti-American.'

The chuckle that accompanied those words threw her completely, its soft, throaty humour exuding every bit as much of magnetic appeal as that disconcerting smile.

'You needn't,' retorted Sian sharply, anger reawakening in her for having momentarily responded to his blatant use of sex appeal—because that was no more than what it had amounted to. 'I'd say the same thing to an English person speaking gibberish.'

'Don't they use the term "ground rules" in games like cricket?' he asked innocently.

'That wasn't what I didn't understand,' retorted Sian impatiently.

'I guess it must have been us being a team, then. So why don't we both go back to our seats and I'll explain?'

With a shrug of resignation, Sian turned and walked back to the chair she had so recently leapt from in fury.

Charming, Anna had called him, she remembered, her eyes examining the tall, lithe figure returning to the other seat—about as charming as a snake, she warned herself sharply.

'What exactly did you mean—about us being a team?' she asked, confused to hear the unintended aggression that had crept into her tone. 'I probably know even less about publishing than you do.'

'You certainly have a way with words, Sian—I guess you see us as the blind leading the blind.' His tone was surprisingly lacking in censure.

'Let's just say I can't imagine anyone in his right mind teaming up with me as a way of stepping into Wally's shoes,' stated Sian stiffly, half of her firmly convinced this was an elaborate leg-pull.

'I doubt if anyone could stroll in here and step into Wally's shoes,' he informed her quietly. 'Or Simon Porter's. Though the senior staff have convinced me that it's Mr Porter's shoes most urgently in need of filling right now——'

'You're going to do Simon's job?' gasped Sian.

'I'll be more of a puppet—with others pulling the strings. As I've had strongly pointed out to me, it's the area in which I can be of most use, and one which would give me a good working insight of the company."

Sian swallowed—hard. There was nothing she could think of to say.

'You were his assistant for almost eight months.' His tone was coaxing. 'And the senior staff, whose suggestion this was, have promised their full support. So, do you agree to teaming up with me?'

'Have I any choice?' She gave a groan the instant the words were out. 'I didn't really mean it like that! What I meant was . . . oh, heck! Between us we could turn away a budding Hemingway—or do something equally ghastly!'

To her relief, and utter surprise, he threw back his head and laughed—a rich, full-blooded roar of pure delight.

'Sian, we'll have the real professionals monitoring our every move!'

'If that's the case, there's a mountain of reading for them to get through,' she said with a sigh. 'For some months now, Simon's entrusted me with weeding out the dross— manuscripts that by no stretch of any imagination could ever be published. Of course, I had to pass a lot of the dross on to him—just in case.'

'And?' he murmured, intrigued.

'He'd get a bit peeved with me at times . . . I used to make two piles, one with those I felt would interest him, the other with manuscripts I felt I should have rejected, but hadn't the nerve to—it would be terrible to make a mistake like that.'

'How often might you have made it?'

'Never—that's what used to peeve Simon. He always said I should have more faith in my own judgement,' she finished hesitantly.

He said nothing, his eyes were on her file, still open

before him.

'I see you have an honours degree in English Literature,' he stated eventually.

'Yes, but that doesn't automatically mean I'd be good at this job!' she exclaimed dismissively, wondering what it was on her file now claiming his undivided attention.

'I see this is your first job.'

'Yes,' she replied, tension creeping into her slim body. Here we go, she added silently, quickly reminding herself that twenty-three was hardly an advanced age to have started work.

'My, you've certainly had some schooling! Even this hick Yankee recognises the names of these establishments.' His eyes rose, the cool mockery unmistakable in them. 'What have I as a team-mate—a member of the moneyed aristocracy?'

'And I suppose you, poor devil, had to work your fingers to the bone to get through law school!' she retorted angrily.

'*Touché*, babe,' he countered. The deliberately insulting use of an endearment and his chilling tone made her think twice—and she discarded her scathing words of objection. 'This explains one thing, though,' he continued in that same, frigid tone. 'It takes more guts to lose your temper and risk getting fired when you're relying on the pay-cheque that comes at the end of each month.'

It was on the tip of Sian's tongue to inform him precisely how much she relied on that pay-cheque to which he had referred with such contempt. It was the way she felt inclined to express herself that silenced her—the black scowl now marring those handsome features warned her that unemployment would be a virtual certainty were she to continue.

CHAPTER TWO

'THE toasted sandwiches will be along in a minute,' announced Anna Walker, depositing two cups of coffee on the table at which Sian sat.

'Thanks. How much do I owe you?' asked Sian, dragging her mind away from the glum morass of thoughts that now constantly besieged it.

'My treat,' smiled Anna, though a small frown creased her brow as she took a seat. 'Mind you, I've a feeling it would take quite a bit more than treating you to a meagre lunch to cheer you up. Are things still as bad as ever between you and Nick?'

Sian shrugged before taking a sip from her cup. What was the use in saying anything? As was practically every other female in the employ of Sinclair Lawson, Anna was no doubt already half in love with the creep. And the men all seemed to regard him as the greatest thing since sliced bread.

'Sian, my office adjoins yours—I'd have to be blind not to notice,' pointed out Anna, her expression sympathetic.

'Notice what?' muttered Sian, knowing she desperately needed someone to confide in and resenting that part of her that always held back. She liked Anna. She had taken to the gentle, dark-haired girl's open friendliness right from the start. Since Simon's stroke, and more particularly since Nicholas Sinclair's arrival, they had taken to lunching together on a fairly regular basis, interrupted only by Anna's frantic bout of flat-hunting the previous week.

'That despite Nick's unquestionable charm, he seems to

spend rather a lot of his time quite deliberately goading you,' stated Anna quietly.

'There's no "seems" about it,' retorted Sian bitterly. 'He's determined to goad me into handing in my notice . . . and I've no intention of giving him the satisfaction of doing so.'

'Sian, surely if he wanted to be rid of you, he'd have fired you weeks ago?' murmured Anna, unsuccessfully trying to mask her amusement. 'When he does succeed in making you lose your temper, you're hardly restrained in the way you let rip! One of the bright sparks on the second floor has christened the pair of you "the lovebirds", and it's beginning to catch on.'

'I'm glad someone finds it amusing,' snapped Sian, all her pent-up bitterness from the past three weeks now coming to the fore. 'Nick won't fire me—he wants me to do his dirty work for him by resigning.' She broke off as the sandwiches arrived. 'He's never forgiven me for those remarks I made the day he arrived—not that he's ever given me a chance to explain them,' she continued bitterly. 'And he won't fire me because I once told him that if he'd had any guts he would have done so immediately.'

'That pig Lloyd has a lot to answer for!' exclaimed Anna angrily. 'Sian—is your job really this important to you?' she added tentatively.

'Yes, and not only because my pride refuses to give in.' She hesitated fractionally, then continued, 'There's the fact that I really enjoyed my work—until that creep arrived. Then there's the very pertinent fact that I happen to need the money.'

There was unmistakable surprise in Anna's eyes before she hastily lowered them.

'That hadn't occurred to me,' she began uncomfortably,

then gave a tentative smile. 'Mind you, I've known you for what—nine months now? Yet I can't honestly say I really know you . . .' Her words petered to a halt as embarrassment began clouding her face.

'Anna, would it surprise you to hear that, apart from my cousin Toby, you're about the nearest thing I have to a friend?' murmured Sian, startling herself with those words almost as much as she did the girl opposite her.

'Surprise would be putting it mildly!' exclaimed Anna. 'Sian . . . I just don't understand.'

'You would if you knew my background, which is probably a trifle weird by most standards,' sighed Sian, picking up her sandwich and hesitating before taking a bite, as a thought suddenly struck her. 'Anna, I meant to ask—did you get that flat you were after?'

Anna's eyes widened in surprise at the sudden switch in the conversation. She shook her head glumly. 'I'll not bore you with the details, but it's back to trudging the streets again for me—in fact I'll be *on* the streets if I don't find something within the next couple of weeks. Oh, how I loathe flat-hunting!'

'Perhaps madam would be interested in a desirable three-bedroomed, two-bathroomed property in Knightsbridge,' murmured Sian, her tone teasing, though her eyes were watchful.

'Madam would be highly interested, had she won the pools,' said Anna ruefully.

'Actually, I'm serious,' Sian told her. 'I rattle around in my place like a pea in a beanpod . . .'

'Sian, I can't tell you how grateful I am for the offer— it's very sweet of you,' sighed Anna. 'But there's no way I could afford even half the rent for a place in Knightsbridge.'

'It isn't rented—I own it,' said Sian quietly. 'It's one of the reasons I need my job so desperately. I've realised for some time now that the only answer is to get someone in to share with the running costs. The only thing is the idea of sharing with a complete stranger filled me with dread—even though the place is big enough for two not to be living in one another's pockets.'

'Sian, I can't believe I'm hearing this!' exclaimed Anna, hope creeping into her expression. 'But . . . are you really sure?'

'I'm *really* sure.' Sian grinned, pleased to find exactly how much the idea was appealing to her. 'We could at least give it a try. If the thought of sharing doesn't appeal to you—you could always use my place until you find somewhere of your own.'

'Like you, it would only be the thought of sharing with a complete stranger that wouldn't appeal, but——' She broke off, her face troubled. 'Sian, this isn't meant to be nosy . . . but, would you mind if I asked you something?'

'Ask away.'

'You own a flat in one of the most exclusive areas of London, which must have cost a fortune. How is it that you need a lodger to help meet the outgoings on it?'

'If you're worried that I'm offering you a roof over your head out of pity—forget it,' replied Sian. 'The only way I can explain adequately is to subject you to a potted biography.'

Though she laughed as she uttered the words, it suddenly struck her that Anna would be the first person she had ever confided in like this. She gave a small, oddly nervous shrug. 'Oh, well—here goes. My mother died when I was four—a freak riding accident that left everyone stunned— and my father shattered. Dad died just over a year ago, yet it was as though his soul had died along with my mother all those years before.' She paused, striving to recapture those faint, perhaps fanciful, memories of the way he had been before her mother's death. 'After Mother died, I went to live with my father's sister and her husband. Their place had always been home from home to me—I adored my Aunt Evelyn and Uncle George, and I positively worshipped my cousin Toby, who must have been around ten then.'

'Did your father live there too?' asked Anna.

Sian shook her head. 'From then on he just seemed to hover on the periphery of my life . . . though he was the one who made all the major decisions regarding it.' Her face clouded as memories began flooding in. 'It was Dad who suddenly decreed I was to go to prep school as a boarder when I was six. The Hadleighs—my aunt and uncle—just about flipped. They tried everything to dissuade him, but he was adamant.'

'But you could hardly have been over your mother's death!' exclaimed Anna in horrified tones.

'That was the problem . . . she had been so alive, then suddenly she was no longer there. When I was sent away to school, I got it into my head it was because the same thing had happened to my aunt as had to my mother—you know how mixed up small children's reasoning can be,' sighed Sian. 'But Dad had decided I was to have the best education to be had—schools, finishing schools, university . . . I was put through the lot.' She gave a small, slightly bitter laugh. 'Somewhere along the line it began to dawn on me that Dad's only way of expressing love towards me was to shower me with material things—and he certainly had the means. The McAllisters were a pretty wealthy bunch, and Dad had inherited virtually the lot—being the sole male heir.' She pulled a face. 'Like the rest of the

McAllisters—my Aunt Evelyn being very much an exception—he had pretty prehistoric views as to the role of women.' She chuckled. 'When I said I wanted to work, his reaction was to mutter something about getting me a little boutique, or a flower shop—something that wouldn't interfere with the butterfly social life he seemed intent on my leading.'

'I can just imagine the sparks that flew,' murmured Anna with a grin, her expression turning to surprise as Sian vigorously shook her head.

'You're wrong. I *never* argued with Dad. I've never really been able to explain it, even to myself, but from when I was quite small I developed an almost protective attitude towards him. I accepted—even feigned delight with—the jewellery and clothing with which he was always showering me. I found it impossible to be my real self with him . . . I don't think he ever had even the remotest idea what the true me was,' she muttered, almost as though she were speaking to herself. 'I couldn't be any other way with him, yet when he died, I felt as though I'd somehow cheated him. Though I'm pretty sure he would have run a mile from the strong-willed and stroppy person I really am.'

'Only when you're given good cause to be, as far as I've seen,' Anna said, with a smile. 'What did your father die of?'

'A massive heart attack. We learned afterwards that his doctor had told him to take things easy a couple of years before—needless to say, Dad ignored that advice,' sighed Sian. 'Anyway, he left a very detailed will—several large bequests were made to institutions and individuals, after which the remainder was to be divided equally between my cousin Toby and me.' She chuckled mischievously. 'When I say equally I mean that Toby, being male, was to get his immediately—mine was to be in trust till I was thirty. Actually Dad did the same thing with the flats—Toby has the one next door to mine, which he got, deeds and all, on his twenty-first—I don't get the deeds of mine till I'm thirty. I wonder if he saw thirty as the age of reason for women?'

'Surely your trustees will let you have some of the money . . .'

'There *is* no money!' Sian chuckled. 'Toby reckons Dad's financial nous must have been as primitive as his attitude to women. Admittedly, there was a fairly hefty-sized fortune left, but you have to remember, Toby and I were at the end of the queue. By the time death duties had been paid and all the bequests honoured, we ended up with a few thousand between us—all of which Toby immediately handed over to me.'

'I think I'm beginning to get the picture,' gasped Anna, shaking her head in mild disbelief.

'You have to admit that there's something slightly farcical about the whole thing,' said Sian. 'Here I am, living in a place worth a small fortune, and finding it a struggle paying the rates! Not only that, I've got wardrobe after wardrobe crammed full of more outrageously expensive clothes than one person could ever get around to wearing, yet I'd have to think twice before forking out the price of a pair of jeans. Heaven knows what I'll do if there's a drastic change in fashion. I'll just have to continue to be exclusively—but old-fashionedly—attired!'

'At least you have a sense of humour about it all,' Anna smiled. 'I've a feeling quite a few people in your position might end up feeling a little sorry for themselves.'

'They'd be pretty odd people if they did.' Sian laughed. 'Tell me, after this heart-rending tale of the poor-little-rich-girl, how do you feel about moving in and easing her burden—even if only temporarily?'

'I could lie and claim I feel duty-bound to help you out—but the truth is I still can't believe my luck!'

'Actually, there's something I'm having a bit of difficulty believing,' declared Sian, pulling a wry face. 'In all this time we've been talking, Nicholas Sinclair didn't once come into my mind!'

'I hate to break the spell,' sighed Anna, glancing at her watch. 'But this has turned into a rather prolonged lunch . . .'

'Sian!'

Nicholas Sinclair had powerful lungs, and he was making full use of them as Anna and Sian entered Sian's office.

'Why the hell can't he ring through—as any normal person would—instead of always bellowing for me?' fumed Sian, storming over to the closed door of his office and flinging it open. 'What?' she demanded belligerently, as Anna, choking back laughter, made her way to her own office.

Nicholas Sinclair spun round the large swivel-chair on which he was inelegantly sprawled, and smiled sweetly at her. 'Oh, there you are! I was beginning to think you'd run away and abandoned me.'

'Sorry to spoil the fantasy,' snapped Sian, her eyes taking in the faultlessly tailored, dark suit and heavy silk shirt, noting with irritation that his clothing always looked immaculate, despite his tendency to slouch at times when seated.

'What kept you so long?' he asked, his concern patently false.

Sian was convinced she heard a click as that knowingly

stunning smile increased in voltage.

'If you must know, I was boring Anna to death with my life history,' she retorted, wondering what his change of mood heralded.

There were days when they managed to rub along almost amiably—infrequent days, of which this had certainly not been one—though the smile indicated this could change. That it was he who more often than not dictated the tone of the mood between them was something she had come to accept with a grudging fatalism.

'No doubt a harrowing tale of a poor-little-rich-girl,' he drawled, the smiling clicking off as he obviously had second thoughts regarding any improvements on today's atmosphere.

'Am I right in assuming you were bawling my name for no other reason than to locate my whereabouts?' she demanded icily, irrationally galled that he had chosen her own joking words to Anna to describe herself.

'Am I right in assuming?' he mimicked, chuckling. 'Sian, you're a real delight when you're uptight! So *frightfully* British and prim!'

'If it takes being uptight—as you put it—you must find me a constant source of delight,' she retorted wearily.

'How about if we call a truce?' he suggested, his tone now cajoling. 'Close the door and come and sit down.'

'There were some calls for you while you were out earlier,' she called over her shoulder, going to her desk and picking up a message pad. 'Yes,' she murmured, a malicious little smile on her face as she closed the door, her eyes on the pad as she made her way to the chair before his desk and sat down. The one chink she had found in his armour to date had been a slight prickliness in him when she had once sarcastically remarked on the number of calls he received from women. 'Let me see . . . there were four calls. Two of them from a Jill Manning, who sounded positively distraught not to have caught you. And one each from a Susan and a Sarah. Tell me, have you ever had what could genuinely be described as a business call since you've been here?' she asked sweetly.

'Sheathe the claws, baby, I save this number for the business calls,' he drawled, indicating the direct line to his office.

Conscious of having scored a point, Sian decided to ignore the endearment used with the express intent of infuriating her . . . she hadn't finished with him yet.

'Don't you think it would be better to reserve the direct line for your hectic love-life, and let the business calls come through me?' she asked, allowing no hint of sarcasm to enter her voice.

'I'm happy with things as they are—with you protecting me from the calls I don't want to receive—and you have to admit, I don't want the majority of them,' he murmured with blatantly false innocence.

'Unfortunately there are so many of them, it's beginning to interfere with my work,' sighed Sian, wondering if it would be overdoing it to bat her eyelids while attempting to look apologetic. 'Anyway, I gave those three this number . . . I must say, to a woman they seemed quite inordinately grateful.' Her eyes widened as she gazed innocently across into his outraged face. 'Oh, Nick, I didn't do the wrong thing, did I?'

Suddenly he burst out laughing. 'Nice try, Sian, but you've overplayed your hand with all that innocence!'

'I wonder if you'll feel that certain when the phone rings?' she asked, cursing herself for not having given in to the strong temptation to give those women the number.

Much of her pleasure was restored by the momentary flicker of uncertainty on his features, before he straightened from his slouching position in the chair.

'I hate to spoil your fun,' he informed her coolly. 'But we have business to discuss. I hope you hadn't anything much planned for this weekend.'

'Your use of the past tense seems to imply I'll be cancelling any plans I might have had,' stated Sian, refusing to react. Simon had made it clear from the start that hers would be no ordinary nine to five job, though the occasions which had entailed her working during evenings and weekends had been few.

'You catch on quickly,' he drawled sarcastically. 'The powers that be—that is, Margaret, Alan and Bill—feel it's time we earned our keep.'

'Would you mind getting to the point?' snapped Sian. 'The powers that be'—who did he think he was kidding? He was the ultimate power around here, and his voracious appetite for knowledge was rapidly making his initial ignorance of publishing a thing of the past.

'I'm to take Cinderella to the ball tomorrow night.'

'What ball?' demanded Sian, her eyes now suspicious.

'One being given by a guy by the name of Linton——'

'Sir George Linton!' exclaimed Sian. 'But Alan Hunter and his wife are attending that—it's still not a foregone conclusion that Sinclair Lawson will get his memoirs . . .'

'The Hunters can't go—one of their kids has just been taken to hospital with appendicitis.'

'Oh, how dreadful!' gasped Sian. 'But . . . can't Bill go . . . or Margaret?'

'Sian, *we* are going. Margaret's already let Linton know. We're staying overnight, as there's to be a meeting with him on Sunday morning.' He picked up an engraved invitation and flicked it across to her.

Her face expressionless and her mind working overtime, Sian picked it up.

There had been decided rumblings of unease in Establishment circles when Sir George Linton, a retired Cabinet minister, had recently announced the completion of his memoirs. The announcement had also brought representatives of the major publishing houses stampeding to his doorstep—Sir George was renowned for his blunt, and at times maverick, attitude to politics.

But it had been to Simon Porter, a friend of long standing, that Sir George had put out feelers—hinting, while never actually committing himself, that it could well be Sinclair Lawson to whom the manuscript would go. Since Simon's stroke nothing more had been heard, until the unexpected appearance of the invitation Sian now held. It was addressed somewhat vaguely, she noted, to 'Simon Porter's deputy, and partner'.

'Why look so worried?' queried Nicholas. 'You know the background and I've just been briefed on it. The way I see it—as this company appears to have a policy of not touting for trade—all we do is sit back and wait for him to make up his mind. Alan tells me the grapevine indicates it's ours.'

'The grapevine!' exclaimed Sian dismissively. 'All it might take is one wrong word from us for Sir George to turn elsewhere.'

'But I'll have you by my side,' he drawled hostilely. 'To stamp me down should my brash, American tendencies show signs of giving offence.'

'Don't you think it might be safer to take someone else?' asked Sian, tight-lipped. 'After all, the chances of us having a public brawl are pretty much a certainty—something from which this company is unlikely to gain.'

'But I like living dangerously,' he murmured, his eyes filled with goading mockery as they swept slowly over her. 'And besides, I hear Sir George has a weakness for beautiful broads . . . a category you sure belong in, despite all your faults.'

'If that's the case,' blazed Sian, flinging the invitation at him as she leapt in fury to her feet, 'I suggest you select a member of your personal harem! I'm sure you'll find plenty of them only too willing to oblige!'

'Sian! Damn it, I'm sorry.'

He caught her as she was half-way to the door, his hands halting her as they descended on her shoulders.

'I'm truly sorry for that remark,' he exclaimed, his hands remaining on her shoulders as she stood to rigid attention, her back to him. 'Sian, in all our spats, neither one of us has ever offered an apology,' he continued, his breath a soft, rustling presence against her hair. 'But this time I am—I'm sorry.'

'Only because you're going to feel an idiot explaining to the others why I refuse to go,' accused Sian, a strident voice in her demanding that she break free, as he slowly turned her to face him.

'You sure as hell have a low opinion of me,' he said quietly, one hand remaining lightly on her shoulder as the other gently lifted her chin.

Though her head could only rise with the coaxing pressure of his hand, her eyes remained fixed on the curve of his left lapel.

She blinked rapidly, trying to focus her eyes, then gave up. They were standing so close together, her eyes were practically crossing, it suddenly dawned on her. It also dawned on her that the simple solution to this was for her to step back—simple, had her legs not appeared to have taken root where she stood.

'Sian, I guess the time has come for us to straighten out our relationship, when it's come to my not being able to admit you're beautiful without turning it into an insult.'

The hypnotic softness of his voice was washing over her like a soothing balm, tempting her with its seeming offer of respite from the unrelenting emotional and mental pressure that had been her constant companion during these past few weeks.

'It wouldn't have needed any straightening out if you'd given me a chance to explain those ghastly remarks I appeared to be making the day you arrived,' she retorted tonelessly, while doggedly trying to steer her mind away from its minute examination of the fact that he had just told her she was beautiful.

'You didn't *appear* to be making them, bab——Sian, they were coming over loud and clear.'

She heard the anger in his voice, even as she recognised his attempted masking of it.

'Nick, they weren't what they appeared to be,' she sighed. 'They weren't what they must have sounded to you.'

Her eyes rose to his face as she spoke, conscious that his second hand had returned to rest lightly once more on her shoulder.

What she was finding most disconcerting was that her mind, instead of concentrating with relief on at last being offered the chance of broaching that fraught subject, was now dithering around—noticing inconsequential things, such as the firm line of his jaw, the almost exotic thickness and length of the lashes fringing the vivid blue of his eyes—in a manner that was totally uncharacteristic.

'How about if we do a deal?' he asked, a slight hoarseness in his voice as their eyes met, each pair widening on contact, as though in sudden recognition.

'What sort of a deal?' asked Sian, blaming the noticeable catch in her voice on the sudden problem she was having with her breathing.

'That you come to Linton's with me—and I hear you out on the drive down.' As he spoke, his eyes remained locked with hers, his hands sliding back a fraction on her shoulders.

It was a movement that seemed to herald his taking her in his arms, thought Sian in alarm, struggling to concentrate on his words, and suddenly finding her concentration broken by an inordinate desire to let her fingers reach up to touch the gold that gleamed at random in the darkness of his hair like streaks of summer sunlight.

'Do we have a deal, Sian?'

Though horrified by this sudden disintegration of her mind, Sian none the less had the sense to nod rather than speak, aware that any words she might utter would probably come out as a stricken croak.

'So . . . do we seal it?'

The telephone began ringing just as his hands had moved in from the curve of her neck and were sliding upwards, his fingers exploring gently in the gleaming thickness of her hair as he tilted her head.

It was the spontaneous parting of her lips—an action that could only be described as an invitation—that started alarm bells, far more intrusive than those of the ringing phone, jangling through her mind.

'The phone's ringing,' she murmured inanely.

'So it is.' In the instant his hands released her, he stooped and dropped a breath of a kiss on her forehead, then strode to the desk and picked up the phone.

To Sian it was as though freedom from his immediate

presence had brought with it freedom from a spell that had imprisoned her, as her still reeling mind struggled to persuade her that the past few moments hadn't taken place.

But they damn well had taken place, she told herself angrily. Heaven knew how his physical magnetism affected women who liked him, if that was its effect on one who positively loathed him! He was like a snake, mesmerising its victim into submission before striking, she fumed, sickened by the memory of her response. And response was what it had been—a powerful, purely physical response to a magnetism such as no man had the right to possess.

'You see?' he murmured, glancing towards her as he replaced the receiver. 'A genuine business call.' He made a half-hearted, unsuccessful attempt at a deprecating smile as his eyes suddenly locked once more with hers.

It was as though those eyes had their own secret powers that gave them access to her innermost thoughts, she thought edgily.

Just because she had been thrown by the sheer unexpectedness of her response to what was, after all, an undeniably attractive man, there was no need to start sinking to the level of fanciful idiocy over his eyes, she told herself scathingly—while at the same time taking the precaution of lowering her own eyes.

'I didn't really give that number out,' she found herself admitting, much to her own surprise.

'I wasn't sure whether you had or not . . . despite my claims,' he muttered.

It was the uncertainty in his voice, a constraint that she suddenly recognised as a mirror image of her own feelings, that brought her startled eyes back to his.

'Sian, if calling a truce is going to make us feel this darned awkward with one another, I'd rather we just carried on warring!' he exclaimed with a familiar flash of impatience, turning his back on her as he strode to the window and gazed moodily out of it.

'I don't feel in the least awkward,' lied Sian.

'Well, bully for you,' he drawled in a mocking parody of an English accent, his shoulders hunching as he shoved his hands into his pockets. 'I'll pick you up at your place at four tomorrow afternoon.'

'Would you like me to jot down the address for you?'

'That won't be necessary,' he snapped. 'You'd better have the afternoon off to get yourself something suitable to wear,' he added, his hand reaching into the inside pocket of his suit-jacket as he turned from the window. 'On the company, of course.'

'I've plenty of perfectly suitable clothes of my own,' Sian informed him frostily, turning on her heel and making for the door. 'I also have work to be getting on with.'

'I think you should have the afternoon off anyway. I can't have you wilting on me at the ball, princess.'

'I was under the impression it was Cinderella you were taking,' murmured Sian innocently, suddenly over-whelmingly relieved that they were now back to their old sparring. 'I think I can manage to stay awake until midnight.'

CHAPTER THREE

'ANYWAY, I don't know what you're complaining about.' Toby Hadleigh grinned teasingly at his cousin from his prone position on her living-room sofa. 'From what I've heard of Sinclair, most women would give their eye-teeth for the chance of a weekend in the country with him.'

'Just note that, will you, Anna?' remarked Sian primly. 'And remind him of it the next time he claims barristers' chambers aren't hotbeds of gossip.'

Anna Walker smiled, her eyes filled with amusement as they moved from the girl curled up in the huge armchair opposite her, to the blond-headed man sprawled on the sofa.

'I can see why you two want me to move in with such haste—you need a resident referee!' she chuckled.

'But you *will* move in this weekend,' pleaded Sian. She had woken to a feeling of pure dread that morning, but Anna's arrival a couple of hours later had brought an almost miraculous alleviation.

Sian realised that, for the first time since her childhood, she was embarking on a close friendship—a luxury she had too long denied herself.

'Sian, I can't wait to move in,' sighed Anna, gazing round the huge, elegantly appointed room. 'I don't think I've ever seen such a beautiful place.'

'I'll show you around my place, once the lamb's off to the slaughter,' offered Toby. 'The layout's pretty much the same, but I seem to make more mess than Sian.'

'You make more mess than most people,' laughed Sian. 'You can cook Anna supper—we might as well shove her in at the deep end. We have an arrangement,' she told Anna. 'Toby cooks breakfasts during the week and I provide suppers—we each take over all meals on alternate weekends.' She chuckled. 'On Toby's weekends we usually end up dining out—his culinary repertoire is limited to breakfasts!'

'And it's your turn this weekend,' Toby reminded her. 'Admit it, you begged Sinclair to take you, just to get out of your duties here!'

'If it's of any interest,' Anna remarked as Sian waved a cushion threateningly at her cousin, 'I love cooking.'

'Anna, forget about us making one trip for essentials!' exclaimed Toby, hauling his long body upright and gazing across at the dark-haired girl with a look approaching reverence. 'I'll get you moved in lock, stock and barrel by tonight!'

'Watch him, Anna,' warned Sian. 'He'll have you darning his socks before you know it. But he's right . . . why not get it over and done with tonight? You could get settled in in one go!'

'But I only popped round to have a look today,' protested Anna weakly.

'And ended up having to rehearse my beloved cousin in her explanation to Sinclair,' chuckled Toby. 'Hell, Sian, did you really say . . . ?'

Sian flung the cushion at the grinning man.

'Sorry, love,' he apologised, trying to compose his face. 'I know you're not exactly looking forward to this weekend, but I have unshakeable faith in your ability to give as good as you get.'

'Thanks, in no small measure, to you.' Sian chuckled, her

eyes brimming with affection as they rested on the man
who had protected and bullied, cared for and tormented her
for almost as long as she could remember . . . her virtual
brother.

'It's a wonder I didn't end up delinquent—with what
I had to take from him as a child,' she informed Anna, her
smile belying her words.

'I was the most tolerant of children,' murmured Toby
piously. 'And to show what a saintly man I've become
—I'll get Anna sorted and installed by the time you get
back.'

Anna gave a smile of pleasure, nodding as Sian looked at
her questioningly.

'Good!' declared Sian, rising to her feet. 'And if the
going gets really tough tonight, I can always comfort myself
with the mental vision of Toby as removal man.' She
grinned. 'I'm off.'

'What do you mean—you're off?' demanded Toby,
puzzled. 'Sinclair's not due for a while yet.'

'And I intend being on the front steps awaiting him—
alone,' stated Sian firmly, going over to him as he rose
and giving him a peck on the cheek. 'Don't fret, Hadleigh,'
she teased. 'McAllister won't let you down—she'll give as
good as she gets.'

'But I suggest you watch out for Linton,' he called after
her, as she and Anna entered the hall. 'He *really* has a
reputation for having a connoisseur's eye!'

'See what I mean about barristers?' joked Sian, slipping
on the matching blazer to the tailored, navy gabardine
slacks she wore. 'Gossips to a man . . . at least, Toby's
lot seem to be!'

'Sian, are you sure you wouldn't like me to come down
with you?' asked Anna anxiously.

'Positive,' smiled Sian. She hesitated, then pulled a small face. 'To be honest, I'm dreading this—but it's best if I face him on my own.'

'Once you've explained, everything will be plain sailing,' comforted Anna. 'And one thing's for sure—you'll be a knockout at the ball in that dress.'

'Anna, you don't think I've overdone it—choosing that particular one? It's a bit . . .'

'Sian, it's fabulous,' stated Anna firmly. 'And that's precisely how you'll look in it. Have you got everything?'

Sian nodded, butterflies darting around in her stomach.

'Off you go, then,' murmured Anna gently, hesitating, then giving her a quick hug. 'And good luck—not that you'll need it.'

At one minute to four, Sian had been standing at the entrance to the block of flats, her overnight case at her feet, butterflies running amok inside her.

At a quarter past four, she was seated on the steps, her chin in her hand as she scowled down at her feet. Angry impatience had chased away nearly every butterfly.

'Someone stood you up, lady?' asked a gravelly gangster voice.

Sian glanced up startled, then glared. She had noticed neither the sleek white Porsche that had drawn up, nor the man who had stepped from it.

'I thought you said you knew where I lived,' she accused, glaring up to where he stood before her, hands on hips.

He looked disgustingly attractive, she thought balefully, noting the close-fitting jeans that hugged the long line of his legs, and the navy Norwegian sweater that was only a shade or two darker than the deep blue of his eyes.

'I didn't reckon on the traffic being this heavy on a

Saturday afternoon' he replied, taking her case in one hand and yanking her to her feet with the other.

As his hand released hers, his eyes swept down her in open appraisal.

'Let's be on our way,' he said, leading her to the car and depositing her case. 'You have a story to tell me.'

The look she gave him as she stepped into the car was one of pure venom, and she rounded on him the instant he was seated.

'Are we by any chance having a communication problem or, by story, were you implying that I'm about to tell you a pack of lies?'

'I guess it's a communication problem,' he conceded, grinning as he started up the car and executed a high speed U-turn. 'I'm all ears . . . handy little corner-store you have there,' he chuckled, as they drove down the side of Harrods and turned into the Brompton Road.

'Would you mind if we got this over and done with?' demanded Sian, though her mind was obstinately refusing to come up with any memory of the calm words she and Anna had rehearsed.

'I told you—I'm all ears,' he drawled, his eyes amused as they flickered momentarily towards hers.

'I'd lost my temper——' she began. That definitely was not her prepared opening line, she thought frustratedly.

'You're kidding me!'

'Pull over—I'm getting out!'

'OK, OK—I'll not open my mouth till you've had your say. But, Sian . . . please don't yell again like that. It distracts me, and I need all my concentration driving on the wrong side of the road.'

'Oh, no, I don't believe this!' groaned Sian. 'Let me drive.'

'No—I'll be fine . . . just as long as you don't yell at me,' he replied, in a voice distorted by the laughter he was trying so unsuccessfully to suppress.

Determined to get her explanation over and done with, Sian took a calming breath and tried once again.

'I'd lost my temper with a man who happens to take a juvenile delight in sexually harassing any female unfortunate enough to come within a mile of him.'

'An American?'

'Of course he wasn't an American! Anyway, I thought you were going to keep quiet until I'd finished,' snapped Sian, then began silently praying as he took a roundabout at high speed. 'You're supposed to give way to the right!' she gasped.

'If you want to back-seat drive, you can ride in the trunk,' he retorted.

'We call it a boot here.'

'Whatever it's called—you got the message.' He chuckled as she glared at him. 'OK—from now on I'll not say another word.'

'All right . . . the reason I was seemingly making anti-American remarks was because . . . I was putting the words into his mouth . . . sort of.' She paused, desperately trying to bring some coherence to her garbled thoughts, acutely aware of how feeble she must sound to him—a point the look he flashed her expressed most eloquently, though he didn't utter a word. 'Heck, I can't remember exactly what had been said now!' she exclaimed. 'He'd made a remark about women finding you attractive . . . the point being that no woman in her right mind would even give him the time of day . . . so, I think that's when I said something about your arrival being likely to put his nose out of joint . . . make him envious. To really rub salt in his wounds,

I said you'd be able to take your pick of the women.'

This was most definitely not what had been rehearsed, she realised uncomfortably, as the disjointed words tumbled from her.

'Then I reminded him of a saying about American men—actually, I think it was directed at American soldiers during the war—meaning that those would be the sentiments of someone like him . . . you know, someone as inadequate as he is.' And a nice little hash she had made of that, she told herself glumly, as a silence fell between them.

'Sian?'

'Yes.'

'Am I allowed to speak now?'

'Very funny!'

'That's pretty much what Alan and Margaret told me. Like you, they didn't mention the guy's name.'

'His name's immaterial,' retorted Sian. 'What I'd like to know, though, is why—if you knew all along I'd not been guilty of a rabidly anti-American tirade—you've been acting as though I were!'

'I haven't. It's just that, with us, the sparks seem to fly.'

'If you think I'll believe that, you're mad!' retorted Sian furiously.

'You don't think sparks fly between us?' he asked in amazement. 'You've just called me a liar. What do you expect me to do—sit back and purr like a pussycat?'

'You can do what you damn well please,' snapped Sian. 'But you *are* a liar if you won't admit that you deliberately rub me up the wrong way whenever you get an opportunity.'

'And you always give me the kid-glove treatment—is that

it?'

'Of course I don't!' exclaimed Sian impatiently. 'But this isn't a question of the chicken and the egg—we both know who started it all. So don't expect me to sit back and purr like a pussycat either!'

'Sian, I thought all this was behind us. We called a truce, remember?'

It was on the tip of Sian's tongue to accuse him of trying to wriggle out of the tight spot in which her logic had placed him. She bit back the words. The way they were going, without a truce they would be at one another's throats before the day was out.

'I remember,' she sighed, and found herself thrown by a sudden memory of his hands in her hair, and the disturbing softness in his voice as he had suggested sealing their deal.

She gave a quick toss of her head, as though tossing aside the memory.

'Do you really think we'll get Sir George's memoirs?' she asked, determined to make an attempt at amenability.

'If the rumours are to be believed,' he replied, 'By the way—I've given Peter Lloyd a verbal warning that one more complaint and he's looking for another job.'

'How did you know it was him?' asked Sian quietly, surprised most of all by the underlying anger in his tone.

'Men like that tend to give themselves away. To give him his due, he did try to come to your rescue—while making darned sure he kept himself covered.'

'But why did you imply to me you didn't know who he was just now?' asked Sian, puzzled.

'I don't know,' he sighed. 'But I do know how perplexing I find your attitude—and that of practically everyone else at Sinclair Lawson. There are women around who desperately need their jobs—and it's guys like that who manipulate them . . .'

'Nick, there's no question of Peter Lloyd having any power with which to manipulate anyone,' she pointed out gently. 'He's just juvenile and rather pathetic.'

'That's often the type who, if given power, uses it to coerce women! I came across that sort soon after I left law school—I found it sickening. I vowed then that no working environment in which I had any say would ever be guilty of accommodating such men. It upsets me that Wally didn't sit on him.'

'Wally, being a very gentle and caring man, tended to judge others by himself,' sighed Sian. 'Did you know him well?'

'Not as well as I'd have liked to. He was my godfather, but his trips back to the States weren't that frequent.' He chuckled. 'My father always says Wally's attitude to London was that of a man with a beautiful mistress—he was scared to leave her too long in case she wouldn't be there when he returned.'

'Yet he chose to be buried in America,' said Sian.

'It was his last gesture of friendship to my father. The first time in my life I saw Dad in tears was when he heard Wally had asked to be buried in Boston. They were inseparable as boys, and they corresponded weekly right up till Wally's death. But, you see, my father was the sole survivor of a plane crash when he was about eighteen or nineteen—and he's never been on a plane since. Wally had only asked to be buried in Boston if he died before Dad—he knew Dad would have made the journey over here, no matter what it cost him emotionally, if he hadn't. As you say, Wally was a very gentle, caring man.'

'I didn't realise you were from Boston—I thought you were a New Yorker,' murmured Sian, then smiled at the theatrically pleading look her remark elicited.

'Boy, do you have a lot to learn about Yankee accents, babe!' he growled, in a heavy Bronx accent.

'I'm sorry,' laughed Sian, suddenly seeing exactly what it was about him that her colleagues found so appealing. 'But the only American accent I could pin-point would be a southern one.'

'Which one?' he queried innocently, then reduced her to helpless laughter by drawling his way through a vast repertoire of southern accents.

'OK—I take back that careless remark!' She giggled. 'You know, you should try the stage when you've finished dabbling in publishing!'

'And what makes you think I'm merely dabbling in publishing?' he asked, the sudden coolness in his tone immediately dispelling much of her new-found feelings of ease.

'I didn't mean to sound derogatory,' she protested, realising that must have been exactly what she sounded. 'I mean . . . having trained in law . . .'

'I upped and left it when I acquired a publishing company?'

'No—obviously you had things to wind up in New York,' she muttered uncomfortably. 'After all, it was three months after Wally died before you came here.'

'I'll be honest—I needed to get out of New York . . .'

'Nick, I'm sorry. I didn't mean to pry!' exclaimed Sian, her cheeks reddening.

'I didn't take it as prying,' he replied, with a smile. 'It's always been at the back of my mind that one day I'd come here and take over from Wally. Like him, I fell in love with London—though perhaps not quite so heavily—when I was a kid.'

'Did you really?' exclaimed Sian, the words just slipping out.

'I really did!'

'But it seems such a waste, your training in law—American law—when you intended settling here.'

'No legal training is ever wasted—though I admit the system here is different. Taking over from Wally was something that would happen in the distant future, as far as I was concerned.' He sighed, shaking his head. 'Hell, he was only fifty-seven when he died,' he exclaimed sadly. 'A couple of years younger than my own father!'

Sian was conscious of his eyes on her as he gave a sudden groan.

'Hell, what am I saying? Margaret told me you'd lost your own father shortly before you joined the company.'

'Yes—in fact he died very much as Wally did—a sudden and fatal heart attack, apparently out of the blue . . .'

'Sian, I'm sorry. Let's change the subject,' he said anxiously.

'It doesn't trouble me to talk about my father,' said Sian quietly, though she felt the familiar feelings of guilt and uncertainty that always assailed her when she thought of him.

'Were you very close to him?' he asked gently.

'No . . . the trouble is, I wasn't,' she sighed. 'My mother died when I was very young—something he never got over, really. I was brought up by his sister and her husband. I'd feel more as though I'd lost a father if my Uncle George died.'

'And that makes you feel guilty. It shouldn't, you know—it wasn't your fault if your father switched off when your mother died,' he told her quietly. 'There are people like that . . . I don't suppose you knew Wally was one of them.'

Sian glanced at him in surprise.

'He'd only been married a couple of years when his wife died. It was because he couldn't sit back and watch his closest friend drinking himself to death that my father bought up Goodmans . . . he knew Wally's love of England, and hoped that new commitments in a completely new environment would be his salvation . . . which, fortunately, it was.'

'Did Wally and his wife have children?' asked Sian, stunned.

'No, but I don't think a kid would have made any difference to the way he reacted to her death . . . just as it didn't to your father.'

'You sound rather like my Aunt Evelyn,' murmured Sian, confused by the unsuspected gentleness in him. 'She was always telling me to accept Dad for what he was, what he had become. I only wish he had found the same sort of niche your father provided for Wally.' She glanced at him, her look tentative. 'Nick, won't you miss your parents—living so far from them?'

He shook his head, laughing. 'I'll probably see as much of them as I did living in New York . . . well, perhaps not quite as much,' he conceded. 'I have no hang-ups about flying.'

'So it was New York you needed to get away from, not America in general,' observed Sian, then realised how nosy she had sounded.

'Stop trying to drag my skeletons from out of their closet.' He chuckled. 'If you open that compartment in front of you, you'll find some tapes. How about putting one on?'

She flashed him a contrite grin as she opened up the tape compartment. Apart from a couple of jazz tapes, the rest were classical. Without hesitation, she chose a selection of Chopin waltzes and polonaises.

'You've picked the schmaltziest of the lot,' he chuckled, as the soft, liquid notes filled the air. 'So, Sian's a romantic at heart!'

He really had a most attractive smile, she decided, her eyes furtively examining his laughing profile. In fact, in this mood, he was an altogether most attractive man, she thought, leaning back and closing her eyes, part of her relaxing to the music, while another part pondered over the skeleton she felt sure was in his cupboard . . . *'I'll be honest—I needed to get out of New York.'*

The second side of one of the jazz tapes had just finished as they turned into a tree-lined drive and drove through several acres of immaculately tended grounds to a large, creeper-clad manor house.

'How about that?' demanded Nick, turning to her, his eyes twinkling in the light shed from the house as he switched off the engine. 'Here in one piece and I didn't once stray to the right side of the road.'

'Or even the wrong side,' chuckled Sian, conscious of a warmth that was almost an excitement spreading its way through her as they stepped from the car.

He gave their names to the butler who opened the door, turning conspiratorially and giving Sian a broad wink as a uniformed maid was summoned to take their luggage.

'Sir George is expecting you, Mr Sinclair,' murmured the butler. 'He was wondering——'

'Are you Nicholas Sinclair—of Sinclair Lawson?' called out a breathless voice. It came from a vivacious, auburn-haired woman, racing down the huge staircase to the left of them.

'I am,' responded Nick, amusement flickering in his eyes as the woman came to a halt beside him.

'Marvellous! I'm Beverley Grade—Sir George's daughter.' She was still trying to catch her breath as she stretched out her hand.

'And this is Sian McAllister, my . . . colleague.'

Sian found her hand taken in a firm, friendly clasp.

'I'm sorry to pounce on you both like this,' apologised Beverley Grade, smiling. 'But Dad's been panicking somewhat, demanding to see you the moment you arrived.'

'Why the panic?' asked Nick easily.

'He's had a touch of flu for the past couple of days,' sighed the woman. 'And he tends to be a bit of a hypochondriac when he's not feeling well,' she added apologetically. 'To be honest, he's impossible. Refuses to see a doctor, while convincing himself he's about to breathe his last. At the moment he has a bee in his bonnet about handing his manuscript over to you.'

'Perhaps it would be a good idea for us to see him right away, Mrs Grade,' murmured Nick, smiling.

'Oh, would you? But please, call me Beverley—and wouldn't you like to freshen up first?'

Sian shook her head. Despite her joking apologies, Beverley Grade was obviously worried. 'There's no point in keeping him waiting,' she murmured.

'That is sweet of you,' exclaimed the woman gratefully. 'He's in his study.'

She led them down a long, wood-panelled corridor. 'I've been trying to get him to call off this wretched ball since yesterday,' she confided in Sian. 'But he won't hear of it.'

The room into which they were led was vast—its every available section of wall-space lined with books.

At one end of the room blazed a huge open fire, in front of which sat a large, heavily built man, probably in his late sixties.

He rose as they entered, his slightly flushed face bathed in a smile of welcome.

'Daddy—it's Nicholas Sinclair and Sian McAllister from the publishing house.'

'Good to see you both!' he exclaimed, his eyes twinkling with appreciation as they settled on Sian. 'So, you're Porter's little assistant, are you?' His chuckle immediately deteriorated into a racking bout of coughing.

'You sound dreadful, darling,' gasped his daughter, her attractive face anxious as she took his arm. 'You really should let me call a doctor.'

Sir George pulled a face at her as he sat down, then winked mischievously at Sian, only to begin coughing again.

'Damned cough!' he complained, rubbing impatiently at his chest. 'I'll see a quack in the morning if it hasn't eased by then,' he conceded, patting his daughter's hand. 'I must say, this is a damned nuisance—I'd have enjoyed a trip round the floor with you this evening,' he complained, smiling ruefully at Sian.

'There's nothing much wrong with you,' teased his daughter, her relief obvious as she affectionately ruffled his hair. 'Still flirting as outrageously as ever.'

'That's one of the perks that comes with age,' murmured Sir George innocently. 'I bet young Sinclair here has to watch his p's and q's . . . or are the pair of you in love?'

'Daddy!' groaned Beverley, flashing Sian an apologetic look.

'I'm still at the stage of watching my p's and q's,' chuckled Nick, not in the least put out.

'Something which I'd guess doesn't come too easily to you,' responded Sir George with a sympathetic grin. 'I'm sorry to have had you dragged in here the moment you set foot over the threshold, but I suppose you realise I want Sinclair Lawson handling my autobiography. I'd have dealt with it sooner, if it hadn't been for poor old Porter's stroke.' He sighed. 'But Lizzie, his wife, tells me there's little chance of him getting back into harness in the foreseeable future, poor devil.' He gazed unhappily into the fire, then turned to his daughter. 'Beverley, why don't you take Miss McAllister——'

'Sian . . . please,' smiled Sian.

'Why don't you show Sian her room, while I fill in young Sinclair here with a few details?'

Sian looked enquiringly at Nick, who nodded.

'Perhaps we could have a little trip round the floor later, if you feel better,' she said to the elderly man.

'What, and deafen you by spluttering down your ear?' answered Sir George ruefully. 'No, but the pair of you could nip in later and have a nightcap with me—I'll look forward to that.'

'It's that cough that worries me—it seems to be getting worse,' fretted Beverley, leading Sian up the stairs and through a maze of corridors. 'The trouble is, he reacts to a mild headache in the same way as he would to excruciating pain—it's impossible to judge how bad he actually feels.'

'At least he's agreed to see a doctor tomorrow,' said Sian, as they came to a halt, sensing how deeply anxious this friendly and likeable woman was.

'Knowing him, he'll try to wriggle out of it,' sighed Beverley, opening the door before them. 'Good—your things are here. If you need anything, just give me a shout.

Mike, my husband, and I are a couple of doors down, on the right.' She glanced at her watch, her eyes widening. 'I suppose we ought to get a move on—the festivities are due to start in less than an hour.'

Once alone, Sian unpacked her things, eyeing the evening dress she and Anna had selected with decided uncertainty, before making her way to the adjoining bathroom for a quick shower.

Unable to ignore the slight tremor in her hands as she made up, she was forced to examine the odd feeling—an almost nervous anticipation—gripping her. A feeling uncomfortably akin to the sick tension she had usually experienced before sitting exams, she realised, beginning to brush her hair with slow, rhythmic strokes in an attempt to calm herself.

Though her hair now gleamed in the soft glow of light, the tension remained steadfastly intact.

It was that damned dress, she told herself, slamming down the brush with an exclamation of impatience. She slipped the offending garment off its hanger and stepped into it, her face registering displeasure as she inspected her svelte reflection in the mirror. Somehow it just wasn't her, she thought miserably, regretting what she now considered her recklessness in selecting it.

The dress was a starkly simple, black sheath—bared at one shoulder, its fine silk crêpe moulding to the softly rounded contours of her body—accentuating each curve with the voluptuous silkiness of a second skin.

It was the slit up the side that caused her most trepidation, she realised, frowning as she stepped into high-heeled black sandals. One incautious stride and she would be displaying leg practically to her thigh!

With a sigh she opened the jewel case resting on the

dressing-table, gazing down at the sparkling set of matching necklace, bracelet and earrings in diamonds and sapphires. She donned the necklace and bracelet, a surprisingly impish grin suddenly lightening the tension from her features as she gazed down at the remaining ear-rings. She might as well wear the whole set, she decided with a chuckle, sweeping up her hair and securing it with a tortoiseshell comb before inserting the drop ear-rings.

'It's into the bank vaults for you soon, my lovelies,' she murmured. The insurance on all the jewellery her father had given her would run out in a few weeks. She had reeled in disbelief on receiving details of the insurance premium —by no stretch of anyone's imagination would she ever be able to afford even a fraction of it.

With a shrug, she turned from the mirror and began practising taking mincingly small steps across the room.

'Come in,' she called out, her face lightening at the light tap on the door—she could do with Beverley Grade's opinion.

'I need your advice . . .' Her words petered away as Nicholas Sinclair stepped through the opening door and into the room, his tall, dinner-suited figure silhouetted sharply against the stark white of the wall.

'What sort of advice?' he asked, a slow smile of appreciation curving his mouth, duplicating the expression in the eyes that unhurriedly swept her body.

'I thought you were Beverley!' exclaimed Sian, annoyed to find herself reacting pleasurably to his open appreciation.

'And my advice wouldn't be acceptable?' he responded, with the merest hint of mockery, his eyes narrowing as he leaned back against the wall, his thumbs hooked into the pockets of his trousers.

Though irritated by such utter relaxation in the face of

her own discomfort, Sian managed to smile sweetly.

'Beggars can't be choosers,' she purred. 'It's just that I'm not sure how long a stride I can afford to take.' Her deliberate intention to confuse was rewarded by his look of bewilderment.

'I believe we're having another communication problem,' he stated cautiously.

'I was merely worried about showing too much leg,' she murmured innocently, fully aware that, from where he so comfortably lounged, he could have no idea of the revealing slit down the side of her dress.

'We still have a problem,' he drawled, the gleam of amusement in his eyes telling her he was perfectly aware she was being deliberately oblique.

Still with an expression of innocence on her face, Sian began walking slowly towards him, exaggeratedly lengthening her stride.

'Turn sideways, and walk across the room,' he ordered brusquely.

She did so, with the slit side concealed from him.

'Now turn and walk back.'

She complied.

'Are you quite sure you can't take longer steps?' he asked, his expression dead-pan.

'I was merely trying to show you the worst!' exclaimed Sian, annoyed by the distinct impression that he had turned the tables on her.

'I'd be more inclined to describe it as the best,' he responded. 'Though I'd suggest the very smallest of steps when we see Sir George later—I doubt if his blood pressure could take what I've just been subjected to.'

'How did you get on with him?' asked Sian quickly, grabbing the opportunity to change the subject with relief.

'Very well—he's very likeable,' he murmured, giving a small, mocking bow as he held out an arm to her. 'That's why I'm rather concerned about his well-being,' he added, his eyes twinkling as they raked down the slit in her dress.

Sian decided not to remove the hand with which she had so unthinkingly accepted his proffered arm, instead she treated him to the most disdainful look she could muster.

'Now, now—we have a truce, remember?' he scolded, his eyes teasing down into hers as he opened the door.

'I suggest you try remembering it the next time you're about to make a sarcastic remark at my expense,' retorted Sian, hastily lowering her eyes.

'Who's being sarcastic?' he demanded, in tones of injured innocence. 'If the left's as great as the right, you have a stunning pair of legs,' he added provokingly. 'And I'm glad you're wearing your hair up.'

Sian made to disengage her hand, only to find it firmly trapped.

'Don't you want to hear why I'm glad you have your hair up?' he murmured infuriatingly. 'Or would you rather I explained why this truce of ours isn't working?'

'No doubt I'm about to be subjected to both,' she snapped, annoyed with herself for the way she was over-reacting to what was relatively mild teasing on his part.

'We'll leave the hair till later——'

'Are we going to this wretched do, or not?' burst out Sian.

'The moment we have the truce sorted out,' he replied. 'You know, a truce isn't valid till it's properly sealed,' he added, a noticeable softness creeping into his tone, as he took both her hands and raised them to rest against the lapels of his jacket.

'What are you doing?' croaked Sian, her hands remaining

where he had placed them as she felt his arms lightly encircle her body.

It was a stupid question, a hectoring little voice from within needlessly informed her, as her head—as though with a will of its own—tilted to enable her eyes to see his.

'Attempting to validate this truce,' he murmured huskily, his head lowering slowly towards hers.

Sian was only aware of having closed her eyes when they opened in shock at the sensation of his lips against her right cheek. Her cheek was the last place she had expected his lips to seek, she realised in confusion.

Then his hands gently clasped her head, turning it slowly as her own hands were sliding upwards to meet at the back of his neck. As he moved her head, his lips seemed to hover only a breath from hers before moving on to make contact with her left cheek.

Mingling with the almost suffocating expectancy tensing every nerve in her body, and rendering her immobile, was an unmistakable sensation of disappointment.

'Perhaps we should make triply sure,' he breathed softly, releasing her head and drawing her fully into his arms.

She made no move to turn aside her freed head, a feeling of intoxication jolting through her, bringing welcome to the lips that lifted to his and parted beneath the gentle exploration of the mouth that took them.

It was the oddly passionless nature of his embrace that, paradoxically, ignited an unconscious need for more in Sian.

He gave a soft groan as her fingers began entwining in the glossy thickness of his hair, the mask of gentleness slipping from him to reveal a capability for passion only partially released, as the softness of his lips gave way to an almost bruising demand. And there was a sureness in the arms that tightened around her, drawing her suddenly pliant body against him in a fierce closeness that left no doubt of the strength of the desire awoken in him.

'Sian!' he groaned, her name a soft protest while her lips still clung to his. 'I think we're about to have company.'

As she felt her clinging arms removed from around his neck, Sian became conscious of approaching voices, and became conscious too of the total oblivion of all, save being in his arms, that had possessed her.

'Sian—Nicholas! This is Mike, my husband,' called Beverley Grade, as she and a tall, fair-haired man approached. 'I was worried in case the pair of you got lost—this place is like a maze till you get to know it.'

'How's Sir George?' managed Sian, desperately trying to regain her shattered wits, and praying the dimness of the light was sufficient to tone down cheeks she knew were flaming.

'I'm off to look in on him now,' returned Mike Grade, flashing his wife a conciliatory look as the four of them began making their way down the corridor.

'Mike can't stand dos like this,' explained Beverley, grinning. 'Being able to play nursemaid to Dad's a godsend as far as he's concerned.'

'Did you manage to get him to bed?' asked Nick, seemingly unaware of Sian's hand still clasped in his.

'Heavens, no! He never retires before midnight, no matter what,' laughed Mike. 'That's when you and Sian are scheduled to have a nightcap with him.'

Sian found herself glancing up at the man by her side, a sudden jolt of excitement winging through her as their eyes met and his hand tightened fractionally on hers.

'And by the way, Nick,' added Mike, 'there's an American art expert just arrived—Sir George is heavily into colonial art at the moment—his wife says she knows you . . . their name's Fenton.'

'I've heard of a Sam Fenton,' stated Nick, shrugging as Mike nodded. 'Can't say I've ever come across him and his wife, though.'

CHAPTER FOUR

'NICK'S likely to need rescuing from those two any minute—if they run true to form,' murmured Beverley Grade, her expression a shade apprehensive as she indicated the two exceedingly attractive women engaging Nicholas Sinclair in animated conversation a few feet from herself and Sian.

'I'm sure he's more than capable of taking care of himself,' Sian replied. 'What are they—infamous man-eaters or something?'

'In a way,' smiled Beverley. 'They seem to hunt as a team—always making a beeline for the dishiest men around, irrespective of marital or any other status. As you can imagine, they've been known to create quite a few scenes.'

'You should feel relieved they've picked on him, then,' reassured Sian, amused. 'He has no wife to object.'

'I know that, but I thought perhaps . . . you and he . . .' Beverley's words trailed to a self-conscious halt.

'Did you, now?' Sian chuckled. 'Well, you can stop fretting—our relationship is an entirely business one.' Except that there had been nothing remotely business-like in that brief interlude outside her room, she reminded herself uncomfortably.

Her eyes lifted to linger on the tall figure of the American, then drew hastily away, sweeping over the magnificent ballroom in which they stood as a jarring surge of excitement sped through her.

'This must have been a wonderful place to grow up

in,' she suggested to her companion, acutely conscious of the strained breathlessness of her words.

'Oh, it was!' exclaimed Beverley. 'Its origins are Tudor—it even has the odd secret passage——' She broke off suddenly, chuckling. 'Looks as though Nick's decided to make his dash for freedom.' She turned to the approaching man. 'There's a buffet in the dining-room —I was wondering if you and Sian felt like eating.'

'Sounds like a great idea,' said Nick, grabbing one of Sian's hands and tucking it through his arm.

As Sian looked up at him in amusement, Beverley moved to his other side, a gleam of understanding in her eye as she held out her arm to him.

'With one on either side of you, you'll be quite safe,' she teased gently.

There was no more than an instant's hesitation on Nicholas Sinclair's part, then he grinned and took her proffered arm.

'I'd always believed the British to be renowned for their use of understatement,' he told them in tones of mild disbelief.

'Not the Carey sisters,' chuckled Beverley. 'They tend more towards the cavewoman approach.'

'Don't tell me you were propositioned—and couldn't cope,' murmured Sian, her gaze wide-eyed with innocence as it met his.

'I was well and truly propositioned—and I couldn't cope,' he replied, his eyes twinkling. 'But it's good to know I've got you and Beverley to protect me.'

'I'm afraid I'm about to abandon you,' responded Beverley, as they entered the huge dining-hall. 'Dad should be feeling a bit peckish by now—and I know Mike will.' She picked up plates and cutlery from a side-table. 'You'll be safe in Sian's hands while I feed the troops,' she said. 'See you both later.'

'Something tells me she's more anxious about her father than she's admitting,' murmured Sian, noticing Nick's look of surprise as Beverley made her way to the food-laden table that dominated the room. 'It's a pity he didn't listen to her and cancel all this,' she sighed, picking up two plates and handing him one.

'He wouldn't have done that,' stated Nick, grinning at her look of surprise. 'It seems he and his wife always threw a ball on their wedding anniversary—he's kept up the tradition even though she died quite a few years ago . . . it's a little sad, when you think of it.'

'You seem to have learned a lot about Sir George in the short time you've spent together,' said Sian, surprised.

He shrugged, then smiled. 'He's quite a character. Those memoirs of his should make interesting reading.'

The smile had disappeared from his face by the time he began helping himself to food.

'I can't stand buffet meals,' he grumbled, picking up a bottle of wine and two glasses, his plate precariously balanced, as he led Sian towards a window.

'My, those Carey sisters certainly rattled your humour,' murmured Sian, an involuntary smile creeping to her lips at the sight of his now scowling face.

'It's nothing to do with them,' he retorted. 'It's just that it's a physical impossibility to hold a glass and a plate, while at the same time being expected to manipulate a knife and fork!'

His deliberately awkward demonstration of his point brought laughter bubbling from Sian.

'Why is it all beautiful women are heartless?' he demanded, throwing her not only with his words, but

also with the sudden smile that danced across his handsome features—both of which were having a profoundly
disturbing effect on her pulse-rate.

'It's not nearly as complicated as you make it out to
be,' objected Sian, while a sharp inner voice began warning her against this increasingly powerful attraction
she was experiencing . . . they were here on business
. . . business and pleasure never made a good mix, especially
when one of the parties was the boss!

'No?' he demanded, scattering her garbled and anxious
thoughts. 'I'm developing positive hang-ups about eating
in this country. I was invited to a grand dinner the other
evening—needless to say, they served peas!'

It was the expression of indignation on his face that
rescued her, leaving her struggling to keep her face straight
and failing disastrously. 'Nick, the significance of peas is
completely lost on me.'

'It wouldn't if you were an American who believes
that when in Rome you do as the Romans do,' he sighed,
his eyes twinkling wickedly. 'There I was, trying to eat
like the British—you know, using only the back of my
fork—and managing only to get one pea in every forty into
my mouth!'

'Perhaps your hostess would have been happier had
you stuck to eating the American way,' said Sian through
her laughter.

'Perhaps—but I don't give in that easily,' he declared,
his expression dead-pan as he took her plate from her and
scraped its contents on to his.

He then poured two glasses of wine, handing both to
Sian. Plate in one hand, fork in the other, he gave her
a smile of contentment. 'How's that for genius?' he
demanded modestly. 'While I feed us—you can ply us

with the vino. Sian! Stop giggling and open your mouth!'
He waited with exaggerated patience until she was
sufficiently composed to receive the forkful he proffered.
'By the way——' he began, then reduced her to helpless
laughter by taking a mouthful himself and pulling a
stricken face. 'Hell, what is this?'

'I've no idea.' Sian giggled. 'It's one of your selections.
What were you about to say?'

'I wondered if Margaret had given you that manuscript I
brought over from the States yet.'

'Not yet, but she's raving about it—how did you come
across it?' asked Sian, obediently opening her mouth to the
approaching fork.

'A friend gave it to me—an Irishman who lives in the
States—his aunt wrote it. I'd be interested in hearing your
reactions to it. Sian?'

'Yes?'

'What about your contribution?' he demanded. 'The
wine!' he exclaimed, by way of explanation, as she looked at
him blankly.

'Sorry!' She raised a glass to his lips—only to find his
height presented problems. 'You'll have to come down a
bit,' she informed him, laughter immediately welling up in
her once more.

'As they say—this sure is a small world.'

Sian gave a start, turning immediately towards the
speaker of those soft, American-accented words, and
found herself looking straight into the oddly expressionless gaze of a tall, attractive blonde woman of about
thirty.

'Don't you think you should remove that glass—unless
it's your intention to choke him?' suggested the woman
coolly.

'What . . . ? I . . .' stammered Sian, the words bringing her gaze back to Nick—still accommodatingly stooped, with the glass she held clamped uncomfortably against his lips.

As their eyes met he raised a single, quizzical brow—an action that left them both struggling with laughter.

'Sorry about that,' murmured Nick to the woman, depositing the plate and removing both glasses from Sian as he fought to regain composure. 'I didn't know you had an American friend here,' he said to Sian, returning the glasses to the sill then stretching his hand out to the woman. 'Nicholas Sinclair.'

'My remark on the smallness of the world was directed at you,' stated the woman, no hint of humour in her voice as she ignored the proffered hand. 'We've met before.'

'We have?' puzzled Nick, his hand dropping to his side. 'Of course, you're Mrs Fenton,' he added, as though suddenly remembering. 'How are you?'

He had managed to trot out the name Mike Grade had mentioned earlier, thought Sian with a small stab of admiration, but she was willing to bet he had absolutely no idea who this woman was.

'I'm fine—but my memory's obviously better than yours,' stated the woman. 'We met at Henry Salinger's—Patty Longhurst introduced us. Patty's a very good friend of mine.'

'It's good to see you again,' stated Nick, with wooden formality.

Sian looked from one to the other, perplexed. This was certainly no friendly reunion of past acquaintances . . . the chill now in the air was verging on glacial.

'I'd like you to meet Sian McAllister,' said Nick politely, his face expressionless.

Sian was treated to a brittle smile as they exchanged handshakes.

'I couldn't believe it when I heard Mrs Grade mention the name Nicholas Sinclair,' the woman told her, speaking almost as though Nick were no longer present. 'So far from New York . . . and I thought he'd be there with Patty, celebrating the finalisation of her divorce . . . I'm sure he's told you all about Patty . . .'

'Mrs Fenton, if there's something you wish to say, I suggest you say it to me,' interrupted Nick sharply.

'You'd rather she didn't hear about the way you've treated Patty?' murmured the woman, the hostility glittering in her eyes a total contrast to the softness of her words. 'How the last thing you wanted was her freedom, because your sort likes to have his cake and eat it without the inconvenience of commitment?'

As the woman's voice rose angrily, Sian felt the tension in the man beside her and saw the pallor beneath his tan.

'The trouble with bastards like you, Nicholas Sinclair——'

'That's enough!' snapped Sian, surprising herself with the anger with which she rounded on the woman. 'We're guests here—and this is in danger of deteriorating into a scene.'

Mrs Fenton gave a harsh laugh. 'Not with Nicholas Sinclair involved,' she retorted. 'He's the sort of man who puts an ocean between himself and any scene that's likely to occur. Remember that, honey, when your time comes. When he ditches you, he won't even allow you the satisfaction of confronting him—he'll be long gone.'

Sian felt Nick's hand descend on to her shoulder. 'Come along, Sian, we're leaving the charming Mrs Fenton to fantasise on her own.'

There was a grim set to his lips as he took her by the hand and began marching her towards the door.

'Nick, please!' begged Sian, finding it almost impossible to keep pace with his long angry strides. 'You'll have to——'

'Mr Sinclair?'

Sian careered into the solid figure of her escort as he halted and turned glittering eyes on the tall, bespectacled man who had spoken.

'Sam Fenton,' declared the man, his face troubled as he held out his hand. 'I see you've just had a run in with my wife . . . I must apologise,' he added uncomfortably, as Nick exchanged a perfunctory handshake with him.

'Why should you apologise?' asked Nick, his tone frigid.

'Because I know Patty Longhurst . . . I can't say I've ever really liked the woman, but my wife just seems to have a mental block where she's concerned.'

'Forget it,' sighed Nick, the grimness of his features relaxing a fraction as he reacted to the man's genuine discomfort. 'But I'd be grateful if you could keep your wife away from me . . .'

'We're leaving right now,' promised Sam Fenton, flashing Sian an apologetic look. 'And I really am sorry.'

With a brief nod in the man's direction, Nick led Sian out and towards the ballroom, his features an expressionless mask.

'Would you like to dance?' he asked abruptly.

'No . . . I . . . Nick, that scene has obviously upset you,' she managed finally. One minute they had been laughing like a couple of children, the next . . .

'You feel I owe you some sort of an explanation?' he asked, the eyes that met hers glacial.

'I feel nothing of the sort!' she retorted, resenting what had seemed almost an accusation in those coldly drawled words. 'But I certainly have no intention of letting you vent your annoyance on me.'

'I suppose I should find your lack of curiosity refreshing,' he replied, anger flashing in his eyes. 'Most of the women I've come across would be dying to hear all the details of a scandal——'

'Which just goes to show what sort of woman you come across—or perhaps that you're given to sweeping sexist generalisations!' snapped Sian, anger stifling any qualms she might have had over her own undeniable curiosity.

'Get off your soapbox, babe, it doesn't suit you . . . Where the hell do you think you're going?' he demanded, grasping her by the arm as she swung round and began to walk away.

'I told you,' warned Sian through clenched teeth, her back now to him. 'Don't try venting your annoyance on me.'

'I'm trying not to!' he exclaimed angrily. 'But if that's your idea of pouring oil on troubled waters——'

'I felt nothing but sympathy for you when that woman began ranting,' objected Sian. 'But you . . .' She shrugged angrily, her eyes accusing as she turned to face him.

'I know,' he sighed, then reached out to steady her as a laughing couple knocked into her. 'Look—we're likely to get trampled in the stampede for the dance-floor here. Let's find somewhere a little quieter,' he suggested, his arm steadying her as he guided her through the throng by the door and around the outskirts of the ballroom to some chairs in a far corner.

'That's better,' he muttered, flinging his tall frame down on to one of the chairs and gazing up at her. 'Sian,

I've never claimed to be a saint,' he stated abruptly, as she took the chair next to his. 'But I've a feeling even saints balk when reminded of times when they've made complete fools of themselves.'

Sian glanced at his face, striving to keep her expression non-committal as she observed his scowling features. The idea of Nicholas Sinclair ever making a complete fool of himself was one she could only regard with a large measure of scepticism.

'Nick, let's just forget the whole thing—pretend that ghastly woman never appeared,' she suggested, forcing brightness into her tone.

'Is that your formula for solving problems?' he sneered. 'Pretending they don't exist?'

'No—I'd say that was more your style,' retorted Sian, her temper snapping. 'After all, you're the one who's put an ocean between himself and his problems! Let's just hope the time doesn't come for you when you start running out of oceans.'

'There's no fear of that,' he rasped, his eyes blazing. 'I learn quickly—there's no way I'll make that sort of mistake twice.'

For a moment they glared at one another in hostile silence, then his shoulders sagged.

'But I guess you're right—I took the coward's way out,' he said quietly.

'You're twisting my words,' protested Sian. 'That's not what I said.'

'You don't think it's cowardly to wreck a marriage, then leave the woman in the lurch?' he asked tonelessly.

'My opinion's immaterial,' muttered Sian, thrown by the strength of the disappointment suddenly replacing her anger. She scarcely knew the man, she rebuked herself;

he could be the worst heel alive for all she knew. And his behaviour towards her had hardly been endearing, she reminded herself sharply. Apart from today . . .

'OK,' he sighed. 'But at least indulge my ego by allowing me to explain.'

Sian shrugged, hating herself for so hypocritical a gesture when every nerve in her body was primed to hear what he had to say.

Suddenly he was glaring at her accusingly. 'I suppose you've never made a mistake where a man in concerned!'

'You suppose wrong,' she replied, startled into a rueful smile by the unexpectedness of his words. 'My record of mistakes would take a lot of beating.'

'At the risk of having you accuse me of sexism again —you have the excuse of being female, and quite a few years younger than I am,' he muttered. 'But there are no extenuating circumstances for my having made so complete a fool of myself.' He leaned back in his chair, his long legs stretching out before him as he rammed his hands into his pockets. 'I knew her as Patty Emmerson—her maiden name—the name she used when she came to work as a temporary secretary to one of my partners.'

Sian glanced at his profile, its grim sternness reflected in the bitter edge to his words.

'Come to think of it, there's not that much to explain. I was bowled over by her zany, mysterious nature.' His laugh was sudden and harsh. 'With as much to hide as Patty had, it was no wonder she came over as mysterious!'

'I take it you didn't know she was married,' murmured Sian, her sympathy diluted by surprise.

'When a woman lives on her own—when she's free to spend every available minute with you—the last thing that crosses your mind is to enquire if she's married.'

'Why was she on her own? Where was her husband?'

'Living on Rhode Island—where they'd both lived until Patty decided she'd had enough of marriage and wanted to lead her own life for a while.'

'If she told you that——'

'Of course she didn't tell me that,' he cut in impatiently. 'That all came out much later—when her husband had decided to sue for divorce . . . naming me as co-respondent.'

'Oh, no!' gasped Sian. 'Were you very much in love with her?' she asked tentatively.

'I seem to remember thinking I was for a while. There was a time I even thought in terms of asking her to marry me eventually.' He shrugged, his expression thoughtful. 'Then things changed and I'm not sure what my feelings were. I know it put me off when she started talking about marriage—there was an intensity about her that immediately set off alarm bells in me, though I was a little off track in assuming it was solely her eagerness to get a marriage proposal out of me.' He broke off, dragging impatient fingers through his hair. 'Hell, I find it difficult talking about it! She actually told her husband about me before she'd had the guts to tell me about him!' he exclaimed, as though still unable to believe it. 'Heaven knows what sort of a marriage the pair of them had—as far as I can see, she asked for a divorce and he was only too happy to oblige. Very civilised, as they say.'

'They sound like a couple of weirdos to me,' exclaimed Sian. 'And she was downright dishonest!'

'Except that in retrospect I can see all the times she tried broaching the subject,' he reflected. 'By then I was dodging what I thought was an entirely different issue. Then I had to take off unexpectedly to Los Angeles for a couple of weeks—when I arrived back in New York it was to find a mind-blowing communication from her husband's lawyer in my mail.'

'And she still hadn't said a word?' gasped Sian.

'To give her her due, she'd tried a couple of times over the phone, just as she'd tried before I left. I guess I'd become a little paranoid by then—I was getting quite expert at dodging the issue.'

Sian looked at him, puzzled. 'What issue?'

'I'd got it into my head that she was going to propose to me,' he admitted, slightly sheepishly. 'I felt pressurised —to be honest, I was wanting out of the relationship. That was one of the reasons I went straight to my own apartment when I got back, though she'd almost begged me to go to hers the moment I arrived. I guess she knew what was likely to greet me at my place.'

'Oh, Nick, I'm sorry for what I said about you putting an ocean between you and your problems,' murmured Sian, guilt swamping her. 'If that had been me, I think I'd have been looking for another planet.'

'Offering myself to the space programme was one possibility I overlooked.' He chuckled. 'But in a way I can understand the Fenton woman's attitude,' he added. 'Patty and I went everywhere quite openly . . . seems my staff, work colleagues and I were the only ones unaware she was married.' His lips tightened. 'It was only later that I learned she'd let her friends believe I was the cause of her separation—and that I was all set to become husband number two.' His eyes narrowed in unmistakable anger as Sian gave a soft chuckle.

'Nick, you have to admit it's not often you hear of a man being tricked by a woman into believing she's single.' She smiled apologetically. 'The shoe's far more likely to be on the other foot—and the men concerned certainly don't usually have marriage in mind.'

'Talking from experience, are you, Sian?' he drawled, a mocking half-smile on his lips. 'Or merely rubbing salt into the open wounds of my ego?'

'The first man I ever came near to falling for was married,' she informed him, flashing him a hostile look. 'Mind you, I was a very immature eighteen and he—he was an unprincipled creep!'

'If he was such a creep, how come you almost fell for him?' he asked, amusement softening his tone.

'Quite easily,' she answered. 'My Aunt Evelyn says I have the most appalling taste in men—and she's right!'

He gave a deep-throated chuckle. 'And you obviously didn't learn from that first mistake.'

'Oh, I learned—never again to assume a man was unmarried simply because he claimed to be.'

'But?'

'But . . .' She hesitated, then gave a sigh of exasperation. 'You're very nosy.' And she was very tempted to continue. It was his laughter that tempted her, she realised suddenly. Talking and laughing with Nicholas Sinclair, despite their ups and downs, was a pleasure to which she could very easily become addicted.

'Sian, I've just bared my soul to you!' he exclaimed theatrically, grinning as he placed a hand on his heart. 'I've told you of the most devastatingly humiliating experience of my life—of the heart-break——'

'Heart-break, my foot!' she broke in. 'It seems to me it was merely your pride that took a knock.'

'You've yet to learn what a sensitive soul I am—but I bet you can't top my tale for making a fool of yourself.'

'You think not?' she answered, the shadow of remembered pain dulling the laughter from her face.

'I'm sorry, Sian,' he murmured softly, his fingers a gentle whisper against her cheek as they reached out to caress it. 'I was only joking.'

'Number two wasn't merely a creep—he was also a crook,' she blurted out, horrified to hear the bitterness spilling into her words.

'Sian, please——'

'No—it's only my pride that still hurts,' she cut in. 'I'd no right to joke about your pride.'

Perhaps she had been close to loving Roy Simmons —now, over two years later, it was impossible to tell. But Roy's treachery had wrought its havoc with her pride well before her feelings had had any chance to deepen into love.

'He used me, used my father's name in connection with shady business deals, used my credit cards——'

'What—he got someone to forge your signature?' queried Nick softly.

'It wasn't a question of anyone having to resort to forgery, exactly,' said Sian miserably. 'In fact, all it needed was for someone merely to write my name . . .' She broke off, conscious of his puzzlement. 'It's a bit difficult explaining—without practically giving you a potted version of my life history,' she informed his stiltedly.

'History just happens to be one of my favourite subjects,' he murmured, his smile gently teasing.

'Well, my father and I were never what you could call close. I told you about my mother dying . . .'

'What age were you when that happened, Sian?'

'Four. I suppose Dad always showered me with material things from a sense of guilt over spending so little time with me. Anyway, on top of an extravagantly generous monthly allowance, he also provided me with just about every form of credit card there is—not that I ever used any of them. Year in and year out the renewals would arrive and I would shove them in a drawer until I got round to destroying them. I tried telling Dad I didn't need them, but they still kept coming,' she remembered unhappily.

'And this charming character found them—still unsigned,' stated Nick grimly.

Sian nodded. 'The statements were sent to my father and it was a good couple of months before he became suspicious . . .' She shrugged, her words petering to silence.

'So your father took legal action?' asked Nick gently.

'Good heavens, no!' exclaimed Sian. 'His attitude to women verged on prehistoric! He wouldn't have tolerated even the merest whiff of a scandal contaminating his daughter. No, he cancelled all the cards and employed a private detection agency to do some digging to find out to what extent Roy had used his name—then he contacted and warned those concerned——' she broke off, glancing up at the stern profile of the man beside her. 'And you thought I couldn't top your tale,' she murmured drily.

He gave a soft laugh as he reached out and cupped her face in his hands. 'What puzzles me is how someone as beautiful and intelligent as you could be so thoroughly conned.'

'I tend to take people at face value—at least, I did, until Roy,' she replied stiffly, suddenly inordinately aware of his nearness and the tingling sensation his touch brought to her cheeks. 'And as for looks—what do they have to do with it?'

'It's usually the unfortunate plain Janes that type of

con artist goes for. There's usually too much competition around when a woman with your looks is involved, and the competition tends to get suspicious.'

Sian turned slightly, freeing her face from the disturbing touch of his hands. She knew that by most people's standards she was considered attractive—but beautiful? This man's frequent and decidedly casual use of the word only made her feel ill at ease with him.

'I knew Roy wasn't married,' she blurted out, conscious of the silence lengthening between them. 'I felt I could afford to take him at face value. I suppose my first experience had made me over-cautious,' she added, forcing amusement into her tone.

'You mean that by then it practically took a sworn affidavit for a guy to convince you he wasn't married, unless you already knew?' Nick suggested.

'Just about,' she admitted sheepishly.

'So, now, what does it take for a man to prove he hasn't criminal tendencies—once you've seen the affidavit proving he's not married?'

'You said you'd never make the same mistake twice,' she responded sharply. 'And neither shall I. How I go about it is my own business.'

'We make our rules, but there are times we can't stop ourselves breaking them, Sian,' he stated, rising and holding out a hand to her. 'Come on—let's dance.'

She rose, expecting him to lead her to the main area of the ballroom, now filled with dancing couples. Instead, he took both her hands in his, guiding her arms around him under his opened jacket. Then his arms encircled her, drawing her to him till her head nestled against his chest. She felt his cheek against her temple, the softness of his breath against her hair, and a strange intoxication began filling her as her hands became alive to the ripple of taut back muscles undulating beneath them.

As he guided their bodies to the slow, sensuous beat of the music, Sian was trying to clear her mind—trying to get her body to relax from the rigidity her mind seemed to be imposing on it. Of course she tended to be ultra-cautious where men were concerned, only a fool would be otherwise, given her past experiences, she reasoned. But this man was unmarried, and one whose credentials few would dream of questioning . . . Suddenly his voice penetrated the jumble of her thoughts.

'Sian, dancing with you is like . . .' he broke off, his lips moving to nuzzle in blatant seduction against her cheek '. . . it's like dancing with a block of wood in my arms.' His arms tightened in the instant she tried to pull away, the palpable ripple of his silent laughter dispelling her initial indignation, demolishing her protests into weak laughter.

'I was expecting a comparison with gossamer—at the very least,' she teased.

'Gossamer!' he exclaimed in mock disgust, his cheek dropping to rest against the dark blonde of her head. 'My, my . . . gossamer,' he repeated, with a softly rumbling chuckle.

She *had* been about as relaxed as a block of wood, realised Sian, as her former tension began being replaced by a disconcertingly sensuous softness, now threatening to melt her. Just because she was thrown to find herself attracted to him—all right, strongly attracted—there was no need for her to start going to pieces, she reasoned edgily. It wasn't as though there hadn't been other attractive men in her life—safe men . . . except that none of them had ever had the physical impact on her that Nick seemed to be having, awakening feelings—needs almost—that were completely alien to her nature.

'Nick?'

The instant she uttered his name, he drew away from her, tilting her back in his arms to allow his laughing eyes to question hers.

'What did you mean about breaking your own rules?' she blurted out, conscious of having called out his name merely to stop the uncomfortable train of her thoughts and then uttering the first words entering her mind.

He gave a barely perceptible shrug before replying, 'To a greater or lesser degree, we all have our personal rules. And, as we make mistakes, those rules have a tendency to increase—perhaps out of all proportion to necessity.'

'Perhaps,' she conceded tentatively. Her own self-governing, self-protecting rules had practically isolated her from men for some time now, leaving her incapable of coping with her undeniable response to this man. 'But you spoke of breaking those rules.'

He smiled as he drew her against him once more. And once more that altogether disconcerting sensation of melting pervaded her.

'I broke what seemed like a fairly trivial rule with Patty —I mixed business with pleasure, and look where it got me! I swore that was one rule I'd never break again.'

'I can understand that,' murmured Sian sympathetically, while the heady effect of his nearness only increased in her.

'Can you?' he asked softly. 'So, what would you say you and I were doing right now?'

'Us?' she croaked, her body suddenly tensing.

'Us, Sian,' he replied. 'I'm not too sure when I became

guilty of breaking that rule with you—perhaps when I started making remarks about you wearing your hair up.'

'You didn't tell me what you meant—that remark about my hair.' Her voice sounded peculiar, she decided, oddly strained.

'But I know what I meant,' he whispered huskily, the play of his lips, as they moved against her cheek, sending the blood pounding through her veins. 'I was admitting to myself that tonight I wanted to be able to reach up, to free your hair and see it tumbling down to your shoulders . . .'

Sian felt his arms tense as his words broke off, and her breath became a painful constriction in her throat, as she awaited that moment when he would draw her fully into his arms, closing that fractional space between their bodies that would turn their half-hearted attempt at dancing into an embrace.

But his arms remained rigid, maintaining that infinitesimal space between bodies that now seemed to call out in silent protest against such decorum.

'If that's all you want, feel free.' Sian's laughter, forced from her by disappointment and confusion, was strained and breathless. 'Who says you'd be breaking any rule? After all, you're the boss!'

There was a sudden roughness in the hands that wrenched her a fraction further from him.

'Sian, what in hell is there about you?' he demanded angrily. 'When I tell you you're beautiful, you react as though I'm indulging in fulsome flattery! When I admit to wanting to make love to you——'

'Wanting to what?' she croaked.

With a soft oath he did now what she had unconsciously willed him to do only moments before, he drew her fully into his arms—his lean, muscled body taut and unyielding against the soft contours of hers.

'Sian, is there no element of fantasy in you?' he sighed. 'For a moment I allowed mine to run riot. I wanted you —wanted to feel my fingers running through your hair as I made love to you.' His lips were now a moist heat, hovering by the corner of her mouth.

'Did Patty have long hair?' she asked stiltedly, every fibre in her fighting an intoxicated need to cling closer—to turn her head that fraction that would bring their lips together.

'Patty has black hair—cut short like a boy's,' he murmured. 'And no, I don't have a hair fetish,' he added. 'It's just that . . . hell, why did I ever start this?'

'But you did start it,' pointed out Sian primly, while her hands explored the back muscles rippling smoothly beneath them. Then she felt the breath catch painfully in her throat as she detected the suddenly increased tempo of his breathing, and his lips began brushing gently, back and forth, against the corner of hers. The breath she had caught remained trapped in her throat, the pounding of her heart quickening beneath the heavy thud of his, as his mouth moved as though at last to savour hers. But his lips began moving slowly across hers, barely touching them, while his tongue traced the outline of her lower lip in a caress that was somehow far more intimate than a kiss. And it was this caress that acted like a catalyst on her, awakening in her a need more powerful than any she had yet experienced. Her lips parted in answer to that aching need, making known that need even as his own lips uttered a soft groan as they tried to draw free from temptation.

'Sian, if I were to kiss you now, I'd find it almost impossible to stop,' he protested huskily, sinking restraining fingers into her hair.

Suddenly he forced her head against him, his arms trapping her suffocatingly close, and she lay against him, conscious only of the message in the erratic thud of his heart that seemed to pound through her.

'When I said that sparks fly between us, I'd little idea they'd be sparks quite like these,' he breathed against her hair. 'Or perhaps I'm not being wholly honest . . . Sian?'

She leaned back in his arms, her eyes opening to rise slowly towards his, a barely perceptible shiver rippling through her as her gaze lingered for a brief moment on the firm fullness of his mouth, before lifting to meet the almost guarded watchfulness of his.

'What?' she croaked, the only word her parched mouth and numbed brain seemed capable of producing.

'The cat seems to have your tongue,' he whispered, that oddly guarded look still in his eyes.

Her arms eased from around him, one hand coming to rest just beneath his heart where the thudding beat it found there immediately contradicted the disconcerting coolness of his eyes.

'That's just as well,' she whispered shakily. 'I'd probably say all the wrong things.'

'Such as?'

'I can't say—the cat's got my tongue . . .' Her words deteriorated into a squeal of protest as he suddenly swept her off her feet, twirling her in a suffocating bear-hug before returning her to the ground.

'Don't say another word—just follow me!' Laughing down at her bemused expression, he caught her by the hand and led her to the throng of dancers in the main area of the ballroom. Then he took her back into his arms. 'We should be safer here,' he remarked drily, his words a soft breath against her hair. 'After all, it wouldn't do for us to start making a meal of one another slap-bang in the middle of Sir George's fine ballroom.'

Beneath the laughter, there was a decided huskiness to his tone—something Sian found paradoxically comforting, given the battle she was having to get a grip on her shattered senses.

'Sian—how would you feel if I fired you?' he asked out of the blue.

'I don't know. I'd probably sue you for unfair dismissal, though,' she replied, with an ease born of a growing conviction that, of the two of them, she was perhaps marginally the saner.

'But then we wouldn't have the rule of not mixing business with pleasure to contend with,' he pointed out, his chin dropping to rest lightly on the top of her head.

Sian was digging in her mind, searching for a suitably light-hearted retort and finding her concentration hampered by the strange excitement his words had churned up in her. There could be no mistaking the meaning behind those lightly spoken words, but there was no need for her to react as though she were a teenager about to be asked on her first date, she informed herself sharply.

'Nick . . .'

'Good lord—it's the divine McAllister—looking as gorgeous as ever!'

Sian felt as though she had been sledge-hammered from sleep as a booming, familiar voice cut through her words.

'James Smithers!' she exclaimed, turning slightly in Nick's arms to gaze across at a beaming, familiar face —an old schoolfriend of Toby's she had known since childhood. 'Jimmy, what on earth are you doing here?' she demanded, relieved to find herself now thoroughly returned to earth as she suppressed a smile. Asking Jimmy Smithers even the most mundane of questions on a crowded dance-floor was a decided mistake, she thought affectionately, as the tall, always slightly rumpled-looking man cheerfully launched into a detailed explanation of his presence.

Jimmy, she realised, would happily spend the next couple of hours chatting to her, quite oblivious of either his partner or hers.

'Jimmy, you've not met Nicholas Sinclair, have you?' she interrupted tactfully.

'I'm afraid Sian and I have several months' chat to catch up on,' grinned Jimmy apologetically, once he had introduced his own partner.

But not here and now, prayed Sian, in the moment before her attention was caught by the sight of Mike Grade waving at her as he approached across the ballroom.

'I hear you and Toby are at Hans Gardens,' Jimmy was saying, obviously intent on doing his catching up then and there. 'And that you've got him doing the cooking!'

'A domesticated man for an undomesticated woman,' drawled Nick, ice glittering in his eyes as they regarded Sian, now turning in his arms, the words of both men lost to her as she watched Mike's approach, her attention riveted by the drawn grimness of his face.

'Sian—Nick! Sorry to butt in . . .'

'Mike, what is it?' she asked anxiously, as Nick became aware of his presence.

'I'm afraid Sir George isn't too good—in fact, we had to call in a doctor, and he's just ordered an ambulance.'

'Has the doctor made a diagnosis?' asked Nick, his arms dropping from around Sian.

'He's pretty sure it's pleurisy, which should have

been treated days ago. The trouble is, the old boy won't move without seeing you first, Nick.'

CHAPTER FIVE

'SIAN McAllister.' Sian's voice croaked from lack of sleep as she spoke into the receiver.

'Sian, what the hell are you doing at work?'

No mistaking those dulcet tones, she thought, her lips tightening angrily.

'Transfer me to Anna,' continued Nicholas Sinclair, before Sian had a chance to reply. 'Then go home and get some sleep . . . Sian?'

'Yes?'

'Are you OK?'

'Why shouldn't I be?' she snapped. 'I'm merely a little tired, which isn't——'

'Well, I feel like hell. I've every symptom of pneumonia and I'm also covered in bruises.'

Without uttering a single word, Sian switched the phone through to Anna's office.

Why on earth *had* she come to work? she asked herself wearily. Toby and Anna had tried everything, short of physical force, to stop her—yet she had insisted on coming. As though in answer to her question, the face of Nicholas Sinclair loomed into her mind, at first laughing—tender, almost—then freezing to an ice-cold aloofness.

The man was a complete Jekyll and Hyde, she informed herself, annoyed at having to admit to a major part of her virtually hankering after that captivating side of him—a side she had witnessed for so relatively short a while, she could be forgiven for wondering if she had actually imagined it. No, she hadn't imagined it—but the reason she had dragged her weary body here, she admitted angrily, was in the foolish hope that she might have imagined that sudden and savage reversion to coldness on his part.

'I must be out of my mind!' she fumed aloud, starting in surprise when she heard a soft chuckle from the door greeting her words.

'That seems the general consensus of opinion,' murmured Anna, her expression amused as she approached Sian's desk. 'I've strict instructions from Nick to bundle you off home—and I intend carrying them out. My, but he seems to have turned into the most caring of bosses where his assistant is concerned,' she added archly. Her face fell as Sian treated her to a look of pure scorn. 'Wishful thinking on my part?' she asked tentatively.

'Pure fantasy!' scowled Sian.

'You can give me the lurid details another time,' sighed Anna. 'At the moment, you look half-dead on your feet. Exactly what time *did* you get back this morning? I know it was the small hours.'

Sian shrugged. 'I've no idea—I seem to have lost all track of time.' She gave a small shudder. 'Anna, it was ghastly—a cross between a farce and a nightmare. The moment the doctor diagnosed pleurisy, Sir George apparently decided he'd only hours left in this world. His only priority was his wretched memoirs, and he refused to let Nick out of his sight. It seems he was determined to go over every conceivable detail with him before his Maker summoned him, and he kicked up the most terrible fuss in the hosiptal when the staff had the initial temerity to object.'

'I take it he got his own way,' murmured Anna, plainly amused.

Sian nodded. 'Mike, his son-in-law, and Nick were at the hospital all night. Beverley, his daughter, was in a terrible state—with all the fuss her father had been creating, no one got round to reassuring her about the state of his health. She and I spent the entire night drinking coffee. I spent Saturday ferrying people back and forth from the hospital—they'd given up any hope of regulating the number of visitors Sir George had.'

She had spent most of Sunday trying, in vain, to catch up on sleep, before collecting Nick from the hospital that evening.

'Nick had practically no sleep at all, so I had to drive us back.'

'But you didn't get home until the small hours!' exclaimed Anna, puzzled.

'My fault entirely,' replied Sian, her eyes dropping to her desk-top blotter. 'I practically wrote off his wretched Porsche.'

Anna's eyes widened in disbelief. 'I beg your pardon?' she managed, then burst out laughing. 'Oh, Sian, I'm sorry!' she choked, struggling for composure. 'What on earth happened?'

Sian's eyes appeared transfixed by her desk blotter. 'I . . . there was a rabbit in the road.' She glanced tentatively at Anna. 'I could hardly run the poor thing over!' she exclaimed defensively. 'Unfortunately, avoiding it entailed up-ending the car in a ditch.'

It was several moments before Anna could oversome her laughter sufficiently to speak. 'What was Nick's reaction?'

'Several snide remarks—after I'd explained what had happened—about hoping the rabbit was unscathed, given that I'd been prepared to sacrifice both our lives and an extremely expensive car on its behalf.'

'I'm sorry, love,' choked Anna, control still eluding her. 'How did you get back?'

'Nick summoned the AA, the RAC and just about every emergency service in Wiltshire—he has all the attributes of a born dictator. Anyway, they got the wretched thing going—then the fun really started.' Anna's reaction brought a reluctant smile to her lips. 'They'd had to knock out the entire windscreen and, needless to say, we drove back in a howling gale and bucketing rain—the car was practically waterlogged by the time we reached London.' She rose, flashing the helpless Anna an impish grin. 'And now the poor devil thinks he has pneumonia!'

'Sian, stop it!' begged Anna. 'I can't take any more of this! For heaven's sake, go home and get some sleep—I'll wake you for supper.'

Only too willing to comply, Sian made her weary way home—sleep the only thought in her mind.

An hour after climbing into bed, tears of frustrated exhaustion were threatening her. She had counted sheep, sipped a hot drink, tried everything she could think of to induce the sleep her body craved.

'Damn him!' she muttered, angrily plumping already plump pillows for the umpteenth time. If anything, she should be grateful to Nicholas Sinclair for the hefty blow he had dealt her pride . . . for the lesson he had most certainly taught her!

She had seen little of him in the anxious hours following Sir George's admission into hospital. But during their infrequent moments of contact she had been confronted with an icy aloofness that had at first hurt and disconcerted her. Then her mind had still been filled with memories of laughing tenderness, of the excitement—the promise of passion—that had flared between them. Later, the brutal pointedness of the change in him had merely angered her.

If he regretted confiding in her, all he had to do was say so, instead of acting with the frigid reserve he had displayed. And he wasn't the only one regretting confidences, she fumed inwardly; lulled by something she was still unable to pinpoint, she had told him things she would never normally have dreamed telling another person.

Suddenly she heaved her restless body over, burying her burning cheeks against the pillows, as his softly spoken words seemed to fill the room.

'Sian—how would you feel if I fired you?'

The strange excitement that had filled her then sprang to life in her once more. Had her reaction to him really been as blatantly obvious as it now seemed in retrospect?

However much he might regret having momentarily broken his own rules, it could never match her own regret for having so foolishly broken hers. She had dropped her guard—against her every instinct—and she was left with nothing but a feeling of complete humiliation.

'Sian—dinner will be ready in ten minutes.'

There was a momentary blankness in Sian's eyes as they opened and gazed up at the girl gently shaking her.

'Anna?'

'You certainly needed that sleep, you were dead to the world.' Concern flitted across Anna's features as she saw the dark-eyed pallor of the face against the pillows. 'Sian, you look exhausted,' she protested.

'I'll come to in a moment,' muttered Sian, struggling upright.

But after splashing her face for several minutes with cold water, then tying back her hair, Sian knew she still looked exactly as she felt—wretched.

'Hell, you look awful, Sian,' was Toby's tactless greeting as she entered the dining-room. 'Never mind, you'll feel a new person once you've got some of Anna's grub in you—I now understand the term "culinary genius"!'

'And no doubt you've had her chained to the cooker all weekend,' retorted Sian, as Anna entered bearing an earthenware casserole. 'Though I must say that smells utterly delicious, Anna,' she smiled. 'I hope you're remembering my warning about darning his socks.'

'I am,' replied Anna, seating herself. 'And there I'd certainly draw the line—but cooking is one of my favourite pastimes.'

Sian pulled a face at her cousin, who was beaming gloatingly across the table at her.

'Really, Sian, I hope you didn't sink to pulling childish faces during the weekend,' admonished Toby piously. 'Anna's been telling me what a *smashing* time you had,' he added, grinning wickedly.

'You have an infantile sense of humour, Hadleigh,' retorted Sian, determinedly giving all her attention to her plate.

'OK, I promise not to tease,' soothed Toby. 'But Sinclair was right, poppet; the pair of you could have been killed.'

'It's easy enough saying that in retrospect,' murmured Anna placatingly. 'But how many of us have the mental capacity to gauge such things when such a situation arises? Most of us would do as Sian did—automatically swerve to avoid an animal—without a thought of the possible consequences.'

'I wasn't really having a go at her,' protested Toby.

'He wouldn't dare,' Sian added. 'He's still mourning the hedgehog he didn't quite manage to miss about eighteen months ago.'

'I only found it particularly harrowing because you made me bury the damned thing,' retorted Toby. 'Anyway, enough stalling—how did the confrontation go with Sinclair? Bar you almost having delivered him to his Maker, I take it everything is now nothing but sweetness and light between you and the dashing American.'

'Do you, now?' muttered Sian, ramming a forkful of food into her mouth and almost choking in the process.

'Oh, Sian,' groaned Anna, 'don't tell me he didn't even give you a chance to explain.'

'I explained all right,' snapped Sian. 'He said his attitude towards me had nothing to do with that—I just rub him up the wrong way.' She flashed her cousin a withering look as he burst out laughing, then found herself gazing into Anna's puzzled blue eyes. 'If it's any consolation, he's told Peter Lloyd he's out on his ear if there's one more complaint about him,' she continued, attempting an oblique shift in the drift of the conversation.

'That's great!' enthused Anna, then immediately looked puzzled again. 'Who reported Peter's carryings-on to him?'

Sian shrugged. 'No one—he says he worked it out for himself.'

'This Peter Lloyd being the office groper?' asked Toby. 'Sinclair's beginning to sound like a knight in shining armour, if you ask me,' he declared when both girls nodded. 'Surely he didn't give you a rough time of it for the entire weekend?'

'No, he actually managed to turn on the charm long enough for us not to be at one another's throats, but he soon reverted to type.'

'After the accident,' Toby deduced sympathetically.

Sian made no attempt to correct the impression both he

and Anna seemed to have gained. The omission brought her a small pang of guilt, until she found herself admitting she would resort to out and out lying rather than admit the truth.

'Well, Margaret's not going to be too happy hearing that,' sighed Anna.

Sian looked at her in blank incomprehension.

'I think she was pinning her hopes on your having Nick eating out of your hand by now.' She chuckled at the expression on Sian's face. 'With the cat away today, the mice had a meeting—Joel Henderson's definitely suing.'

'Oh, hell!' groaned Sian. 'Does Nick know yet?'

'He was the one who told Margaret on Friday. He's asked her to get the relevant paperwork together for him, though she says he didn't seem in any way perturbed. She feels his view is that a crook such as Henderson would automatically threaten a lawsuit—and that a publishing house such as Sinclair Lawson would always be thoroughly covered legally.'

'And he's right, damn it!' groaned Sian. 'There's no way Simon Porter would have overlooked even the most seemingly insignificant legal implication. I know his methods were often unorthodox, but he was little short of pedantic when it came down to the nitty-gritty.'

'That's not going to get Sinclair Lawson very far in court,' muttered Toby. 'Unless you have watertight verification, you can only publish if all references to Henderson are deleted.'

'That's impossible—the book's due to be launched within a couple of months,' protested Anna.

'This isn't my field, but from what Sian's told me, I very much doubt it will be.'

'Perhaps they could postpone publication until Simon's

You may be the winner of the

MILLION DOLLAR
GRAND PRIZE!

TO BE
ELIGIBLE,
AFFIX THIS
STICKER TO
SWEEPSTAKES
ENTRY FORM

FOR A
CHANCE AT
THOUSANDS
OF OTHER
PRIZES, ALSO
AFFIX THIS
STICKER TO
ENTRY FORM

TO GET FREE
BOOKS AND
GIFTS, AFFIX
THIS STICKER
AS WELL!

ENTER HARLEQUIN'S *BIGGEST* SWEEPSTAKES EVER!

IT'S FUN! IT'S FREE!
AND YOU COULD BE A
MILLIONAIRE!

Your unique Sweepstakes Entry Number appears on the Sweepstakes Entry Form. When you affix your Sweepstakes Entry Sticker to your Form, you're in the running, and you could be the $1,000,000.00 annuity Grand Prize Winner! That's $33,333.33 every year for up to 30 years!

AFFIX BONUS PRIZE STICKER

to your Sweepstakes Entry Form. If you have a winning number, you could collect any of 8,617 prizes. And we'll also enter you in a special bonus prize drawing for a new Ford Mustang and the "Aloha Hawaii Vacation."

AFFIX FREE BOOKS
AND GIFTS STICKER

to take advantage of our Free Books/Free Gifts introduction to the Harlequin Reader Service®. You'll get four brand new Harlequin Presents® novels, plus a 20kt gold electroplated necklace and a mystery gift, absolutely free!

NO PURCHASE NECESSARY!

Accepting free books and gifts places you under no obligation to buy a thing! After receiving your free books, if you don't wish to receive any further volumes, write "cancel" on the shipping document and return it to us. But if you choose to remain a member of the Harlequin Reader Service, you'll receive six more Harlequin Presents novels every month for just $2.24* each—26 cents below the cover price, with no additional charge for delivery! You can cancel at any time by dropping us a line, or by returning a shipment to us at our cost. Even if you cancel, your first four books, your 20kt gold electroplated chain and your mystery gift are absolutely free—our way of thanking you for giving the Reader Service a try!

* Terms and prices subject to change without notice.

Sales tax applicable in N.Y. and Iowa

You'll love your elegant 20kt gold electro-plated chain! The necklace is finely crafted with 160 double-soldered links and is electro-plate finished in genuine 20kt gold. And it's free as added thanks for giving our **Reader Service** a try!

Harlequin Reader Service® Sweepstakes Entry Form

This is your **unique**
Sweepstakes Entry Number: 3L 169814

This could be your lucky day! If you have the winning number, you could be the Grand Prize Winner. To be eligible, *affix Sweepstakes Entry Sticker here!*

If you would like a chance to win the $25,000.00 prize, the $10,000.00 prize, or one of the many $5,000.00, $1,000.00, $250.00 or $10.00 prizes…plus the Mustang and the Hawaiian Vacation, *affix Bonus Prize Sticker here!*

To receive free books and gifts with no obligation to buy, as explained on the opposite page, *affix the Free Books and Gifts Sticker here!*

Please enter me in the sweepstakes and, when the winner is d͟ tell me if I've won the $1,000,000.00 Grand Prize! Also tell I've won any other prize, including the car and the vacation ͏ Please ship me the free books and gifts I've requested with st͟ above. Entering the Sweepstakes costs me nothing and places ͏ under no obligation to buy! (If you do not wish to receive free books and gifts, do not affix the FREE BOOKS and GIFTS sticker

106 CIH BA6F
(U-H-P-08/90)

YOUR NAME	PLEASE PRINT	
ADDRESS		APT#
CITY	STATE	ZIP

Offer limited to one per household and not valid for current Harlequin Presents subscribers.
Printed in U.S.A.   © 1990 Harlequin Enterprises Ltd.

MILLION DOLLAR GRAND PRIZE
SWEEPSTAKES ENTRY STICKER
$1,000,000.00

Harlequin's "No Risk" Guarantee

- You're not required to buy a single book—ever!
- As a subscriber, you must be completely satisfied or you may cancel at any time by marking "cancel" on your statement or returning a shipment of books at our cost.
- The free books and gifts you receive are yours to keep.

If card is missing, write to: Harlequin Reader Service, P.O. Box 1867, Buffalo, NY 14269-1867

Printed in U.S.A.

up to giving an explanation,' suggested Sian, but with little conviction.

'Bill Gardiner's started sifting through the paperwork Simon has at home,' said Anna. 'He's had to spin Mrs Porter a story . . .'

'Hell, I hope he's made it convincing!' exclaimed Sian. 'She's enough on her plate without worrying about Simon being sacked.'

'Sian, stop being so melodramatic,' groaned Toby. 'Sinclair's hardly likely to sack the poor bloke——'

'But he's perfectly entitled to,' cut in Anna miserably. 'It's all spelled out in Simon's contract—Margaret's checked it.'

'And, being a lawyer, Nicholas Sinclair would be more likely than most to apply the exact letter of the law,' added Sian glumly.

'Being a law man myself, I take strong exception to that remark,' protested Toby.

'You needn't,' teased Sian. 'We all know you're just a great big softie, whereas Nicholas Sinclair . . .'

Those words of the night before were in her thoughts as she placed two files on Nicholas Sinclair's desk, then returned to her own office. Had Nick shown the least sign of being a "softie", none of this would have been necessary. She frowned as she glanced at her watch. It had taken a lot longer than she had anticipated, she fretted, picking up the phone. 'Jill, it's Sian—could I have a word with Anna?' she asked the receptionist. 'I've finished, so you can stop loitering,' she told an anxious-sounding Anna. 'I'm just off to Margaret to explain—I'll see you later.'

There was a smile that was part welcome, part surprise on Margaret Fell's face as Sian entered her office.

'Don't tell me you've read it already?' she exclaimed.

For a second, Sian gazed at her uncomprehendingly, then she shook her head. 'That's the very next thing on my agenda—after having a word with you, that is,' said Sian, taking a seat, suddenly conscious of the butterflies running amok in her stomach.

'Nick was most insistent that you read that manuscript today,' Margaret told her, frowning slightly as she glanced at her watch. 'He'll be in soon. What was it you wanted to discuss?'

'The Joel Henderson problem . . . I've doctored the files,' she blurted out, wondering why on earth she hadn't had the sense to plan what she intended saying.

'What do you mean—you've doctored the files?' asked Margaret in an ominously quiet voice. She rose suddenly. 'I was about to have a coffee—would you like one?'

Sian nodded, all at once feeling very unsure of herself.

'I had to do something—no one's come up with anything to vindicate Simon,' she protested.

'Not yet,' agreed Margaret, returning to her desk with two cups and handing Sian one. 'What exactly have you done?' she asked, in that same quiet voice.

'I've merely added and subtracted one or two carbons and memos—and substituted my signature for Simon's once or twice.'

'And what if Bill comes up with the evidence we're all sure exists?' asked Margaret, her tone unchanged.

'I've altered the files vaguely enough to allow for that,' declared Sian, confused by what she was sure was the older woman's negative reaction to what she had done. 'Under the circumstances, I felt Simon should be protected at all costs,' she went on defensively. 'And, unlike him, I'm young and fit and capable of finding other work—*if* it comes to that.'

'And you don't think it will?' asked Margaret coolly.

'I don't know,' sighed Sian, now feeling thoroughly confused. The consequences of putting her job, which she so desperately needed, in such jeopardy were only now beginning to assail her—and Margaret's scarcely veiled censure was the last thing she had expected. 'The way I see it, Nick's quite likely to fire me for one reason or another soon—the atmosphere between us isn't exactly one of sweetness and light. If I'm going to go, I might as well go with a bang, and help Simon in the process.'

'It doesn't seem to have occurred to you that, as your department head, Simon is ultimately responsible for your actions,' said Margaret sharply. 'All you appear to have done is provide Nick with a reason for getting rid of *you*! Sian, don't think I don't appreciate your reasons for acting as you have,' she added gently. 'But you've acted illogically and that's not going to help Simon in the least.'

'But if Nick could be convinced that Simon wasn't acting responsibly before his stroke——'

'If he could be convinced of that, why bother trying to implicate yourself in the first place?' interrupted Margaret impatiently. 'Sian, as far as I can see, you've leapt into this with your eyes tightly shut—without bothering to look at where it might lead!'

It was because she hadn't dared contemplate being incomeless, for even a short period, that she had forced herself to plough ahead with the idea, she thought miserably. That there might be other angles worth examining hadn't occurred to her, so determined had she been not to give herself a chance to back out.

'I feel like a complete idiot,' groaned Sian, taking a quick gulp of coffee. 'Anna warned me I should consult you first . . .'

'Sian, instead of berating yourself, I suggest you go and get those wretched files,' murmured Margaret. 'Heaven knows what Nick's going to say when he hears they're not ready for him. How long do you think the undoctoring process will take?' she added with a wry smile.

'Hours, probably,' groaned Sian. 'I religiously shredded what I removed from them. Margaret, are you sure he'd still hold Simon responsible . . .?'

'Sian!' groaned Margaret. 'For heaven's sake, get those files.' She glanced at her watch, shaking her head. 'If it isn't already too late,' she added grimly.

Jumping up, Sian tore back to her own office, racing through it and flinging open the door to Nick's.

'Late lunch?' drawled Nick, his cool gaze lifting from one of the two files that had caused her frantic dash.

'No, I had to see Margaret. I . . .'

'Sian, is something wrong?' he demanded, rising.

'Wrong? No, nothing's wrong,' she gabbled, trying to get a grip on herself. 'I thought I heard a noise in your office—I didn't realise you were back.'

'I'm back.'

Straightening from the door-frame, against which she had almost collapsed at the sight of him, Sian turned to leave.

'Are you feeling better?' she asked, her concern an obvious afterthought.

'Yes, thank you.'

Leaden-footed, Sian walked to her deak and sat down. She was trying to force her mind to concentrate on the fact that soon she would be out of a job—and the fact that her thoughtless act of bravura had done nothing to protect Simon. But her mind kept veering towards other considerations, such as the last time she had seen Nicholas Sinclair, in the early hours of a morning a couple of days before—both of them soaked and frozen and neither having bothered to make any attempt at conversing for several hours.

And conversation with her was obviously something he intended restricting to the barest essentials, she told herself angrily, opening the manuscript Margaret had given her earlier and trying to apply herself to it.

'Sian, haven't you read that damned thing yet?' demanded Nick from the doorway. 'I rang Margaret and expressly asked——'

'And she passed on your orders,' snapped Sian. 'The thing is, I happened to have other things to do, and I can't read with you standing over me with a stop-watch in your hand,' she added curtly as he walked towards her desk.

'Is there any chance . . .?' He halted suddenly, a spasm of pain flitting across his face. 'Is there any chance of your reading it today?' He spoke as though nothing had happened, but his right hand had started moving back and forth across his rib-cage—a plainly reflex gesture to assuage pain.

'I suppose so—if I dropped everything else. Why the rush, though?' asked Sian, determined to say nothing that might sound like prying on her part. She had enquired as to his health and had received his brusque reply—and that, as far as she was concerned, was that.

'You know what they say about procrastination being the thief of time—it's my baby and I don't want it gathering dust,' he informed her smoothly.

In other words, you're the boss and I'm to do as I'm told, thought Sian, wanting to hurl the manuscript at him. 'I'd best get cracking on it, then,' she observed tartly instead.

'I nearly forgot!' he exclaimed, as Sian pointedly returned

her attention to the manuscript. 'Jack Soames can't make lunch tomorrow, so I've arranged a table for tonight. I'll pick you up at eight.' He turned towards the open door of his office.

His casual words sent a white-hot shaft of fury winging through Sian.

'I beg your pardon?' she managed, through clenched teeth.

'I said, I'll pick you up at eight,' he repeated, his face suddenly creasing once more with pain as he swung round to face her.

'Are you sure you're all right?' she asked, the words of concern slipping out, despite the anger still boiling in her.

He shrugged. 'I'm fine. I take it you *are* free for tonight?'

'That's hardly the point,' she replied stonily. 'While I accept the fact that this isn't always a strictly nine-to-five job, Simon always had the courtesy to give me a couple of days' warning of any entertaining to be done!'

'Sorry,' he drawled sarcastically. 'I'm just an uncouth American——' He broke off, his eyes glinting surprise as Sian leapt to her feet, enraged.

'And you still expect me to believe your attitude towards me isn't influenced by what I was saying the first time we met?' she accused heatedly. 'Because the remark you've just made——'

'That remark was made because it didn't even occur to you to give me the benefit of the doubt—to you there wasn't even a doubt for which to give me any benefit!' he interrupted coldly. 'Something urgent has cropped up in the States for Soames, he's having to fly there tomorrow. He rang me, less than half an hour ago, full of apologies and to suggest a meal tonight. As he's one of Simon's authors and I hardly know the guy, I assumed . . .'

'OK—I'm sorry,' muttered Sian, her tone lacking any semblance of contrition.

'Accepted,' he snapped, glowering at her. 'Does that mean you're coming—or do you require a written invitation?'

Sian's lips tightened, but her eyes remained unwavering on the open manuscript before her.

'Perhaps you should ring Toby—let him know in good time he'll only be cooking for one tonight,' he threw over his shoulder, before the door of his office closed behind him.

Sian's eyes flew to the closed door, wide with astonishment as she wondered when on earth she had ever been relaxed enough in the wretched man's company to mention her cousin—let alone their culinary arrangements. Perhaps at Sir George's, before . . . She gave a sudden involuntary shiver as vivid memories crowded into her mind.

No matter when, she told herself with a dismissive shrug—but trust him to twist whatever she *had* said into making it sound as though Toby were some sort of long-suffering kitchen maid. The mere thought of her cousin in such a role had her clapping her hand across her mouth to stifle her giggles.

It was a pity she wouldn't be able to indulge in teasing Toby over this little gem, she thought, with an affectionate chuckle, but knowing him he would be quite capable of launching into a 'wounded male pride' routine as an excuse to get out of his cooking chores. And no doubt Anna would only aid and abet him in such macho subterfuge—Anna was already showing signs of an unfortunate willingness to spoil him!

CHAPTER SIX

SIAN closed the file in front of her and leapt to her feet. It was a waste of time pretending she was working—or was even capable of it.

She made her way towards Anna's office, her eyes lingering for an instant on the closed door of Nick's office as it passed through her line of vision.

'You don't happen to feel like a coffee-break?' she asked tentatively, popping her head round Anna's door.

'I was just about to have one,' replied Anna, rising. 'Time hanging a bit heavily, is it?' she added sympathetically.

'It seems as though Margaret's been in with him for hours,' sighed Sian, flopping on to a chair. 'Anna, how could I have been so stupid?' she groaned despairingly. 'I couldn't tell you the whole truth when I asked you to keep watch for Nick, though if I'd had the sense to confide in you I wouldn't be in this state . . .'

'Sian, you're only assuming it's the Henderson business he's discussing with Margaret,' soothed Anna, handing her a mug of coffee. 'And another thing, she might be cross with you to your face, but she was full of praise for your loyalty to Simon—misguided and muddled though it was.'

'It had about as much reasoning behind it as a four-year-old would have been capable of,' groaned Sian, drumming her fingernails nervously against the side of the mug.

'Crying over spilt milk isn't going to help anyone,' said Anna firmly. 'You'll just have to try to blot it from your mind for the time being and hope——'

'Hope!' exclaimed Sian gloomily. 'What I should be doing is clearing out my desk! You'll be most surprised to hear that Nick and I parted practically on screaming terms after our working dinner last night—and this time it definitely wasn't my fault. I was actually showing concern for the creep . . .'

'And no doubt that's how you worded it,' murmured Anna, unable to keep her face straight.

'You may find it amusing, but that man will welcome any excuse to get rid of me—and to think *I'm* the idiot who's gone to the trouble of manufacturing a cast-iron reason for him!'

'Sian, snap out of it,' chided Anna. 'You've got to——' She broke off, her expression relieved as Margaret's beaming face appeared round the door.

'Thought I might find you here,' she told them as she entered. 'And you can stop looking as though you're awaiting the gallows, my girl,' she told Sian, giving her shoulder an affectionate squeeze. 'Nick showed no interest whatsoever in your cooked-up role in the matter. Luckily his view is exactly what ours was—that there's no way a man of Simon's calibre would have acted so suddenly out of character.'

'You mean he's not going to fire me?' croaked Sian, the words refusing to sink in.

'I mean he's not firing you and he's seeing to it that Simon's very well provided for financially.' She broke off, her homely face suddenly serious. 'He's offered Bill any help he can, sorting through the papers Simon has at home.' She shook her head as she looked at Sian. 'He's been through those files with a toothcomb—I could hardly say to him "Oh, by the way, Nick, those files might be a little misleading as Sian's doctored them", could I?

Before I forget, he wants to see you,' she added to the cringing Sian.

'And I'd better tell him about the files——'

'You'll do no such thing!' exclaimed Margaret, horrified. 'Let's just be grateful for the way things have turned out and leave well alone.'

'If you're sure,' sighed Sian, rising.

'I'm positive—so, off you go,' said Margaret.

As she reached the door of Nick's office, she hesitated. How could Margaret have been so positive? She could only think of one reason Nick would want to see her—and that was to tell her she was fired.

That conclusion firmly embedded in her mind, she braced herself, opened the door and walked in.

'Close the door,' he growled, his back to her as he stood before one of the windows.

'Please!' called out Sian, slamming shut the door.

'And while you're at it—lock the damned thing!'

'What?' she croaked, refusing to believe her ears.

'Don't lock it, then, I don't give a damn . . . Sian, will you help me get this jacket off, *please*?' Even as he spoke, he was struggling to rid himself of the soft, black leather jacket he wore. His face, as he turned to her, was contorted with pain.

Without thinking, Sian was beside him. 'You just wouldn't listen to me, would you?' she accused, the memory of the undisguised pain in which he had been the previous evening returning as she helped ease the jacket over the breadth of his shoulders. 'When I suggested taking you to a hospital last night, all you did was hurl abuse at me!' Suddenly her shaking hands were dragging the jacket back over his shoulders. 'It's pointless taking this off—you're going straight to the nearest casualty department——'

'I've been to a damned hospital!' he roared, pulling free of her hands and stripping off the jacket. 'I don't know why in hell I listened to you!'

If his words hadn't convinced her he was completely mad, the fact that he had now begun removing his shirt certainly did.

'Nick, what on earth's the matter? Why are you . . .? Hell, what's happened to you?' she shrieked as he shrugged off the shirt to reveal a large area of starkly white strapping against a deeply tanned torso.

'Sian, would you mind keeping your voice down? Or lock the door—we'll have half the staff in here if you keep hollering like that!'

'Nick, tell me what's happened,' she demanded, her voice, if anything, louder.

'The rabbit might have been OK, but several of my ribs aren't. Now, will you get this damned tape off me, before it drives me completely mad?'

'What do you mean—get it off you?' she gasped. 'Nick, don't be ridiculous.'

'Sian,' he pleaded, making an obvious effort to control himself, 'the only ridiculous thing I did was listening to you last night. As I'm not a contortionist, I'm reduced to begging you—will you get this damn thing off me?'

'But they put it on for a reason . . . Nick, is it hurting you?'

'No, the itching is driving me mad. I forgot all about it when I leapt under the shower this morning . . . as it's been drying out it's been driving me insane!'

Sian reached out and touched the wide band of strapping that ran from the centre of his chest, round his left side to the centre of his broad, brown back—it was still very damp.

'It'll hurt,' she warned, her voice not quite steady. 'The hairs on your chest——'

'Pain will be bliss after this, Sian. Just get on with it.'

Disconcerted by the unfathomable expression in the blue eyes peering down at her, Sian moved round to the back of him.

The skin of his back was warm and silken beneath her fingers as she gently eased back the edges of the strapping.

'Hell, Sian, I didn't envisage hours of torture—just one quick tug!' he protested, twisting to peer over his shoulder at what she was doing.

'I have to get something to grasp hold of,' she told him sharply, pushing aside his left arm as she leaned round and repeated the process at the front of him.

While her fingers moved at their task, she was filled with a sudden and irrational urge to let them roam and explore in the springy darkness of hair beneath them, and a wry smile crossed her lips as she imagined his scathing response to such a liberty.

'So, I'm at the mercy of a little sadist, am I?' he murmured, spotting the smile.

'Yes, you are,' she replied, both hands suddenly tugging with all their might and ripping off the strapping.

'Free at last!' he exclaimed, catching her in his arms and swinging her round. 'You're my damsel in shining armour!'

'It's the knights that have the shining armour—the damsels usually get lumbered with the distress,' murmured Sian, battling against the almost violent surge of excitement that had begun racing within her the instant his arms had enclosed her.

'Not when their ribs are in the state mine are,' he joked.

They were standing close together, in a strange partial embrace, and Sian found herself listening, mesmerised, to the thunderous pounding of her heart, noting each thudding beat as it jarred through her body.

'Seems I call on you to get me out of one fix, and you land me straight into another,' he murmured huskily, his arms tightening around her.

Her senses were being swamped by the warm, masculine scent of him, by the acutely exciting sensation of taut muscles beneath the hands that rested, immobile, against his back.

The feelings stirring within her were so powerful, so alien, that her resistance, though reluctant, was automatic.

Her hands dropped from him. 'The only reason I'm not pushing you away is that I'm afraid of hurting your ribs,' she managed, her voice strained and breathless.

'Liar,' he whispered, pulling her more firmly against him as his lips began moving across her cheek.

'I mean it, Nick,' she insisted, her voice less blurred, slightly firmer.

'Push me away, if you really want to, Sian. I shan't cry,' he murmured, his lips now nuzzling the corners of hers.

She took a step back from him, disconcerted to find how easily his arms relinquished her.

'Nick, I . . . heavens, no wonder you were itching,' she babbled, her eyes, unable to lift to his, locked on the brown expanse of torso. 'You've a rash all over where the plaster was!'

'Sian, what's wrong with you?' he asked softly, completely ignoring her almost manic rush of words.

'What's wrong with me?' she echoed, a swift surge of anger deepening the already heightened colour of her cheeks. 'You should try asking yourself that. You're unbalanced!' she accused, anger suddenly running riot in her. 'First of all you treat me like a carrier trying to foist the plague on you! Then you . . . you . . . you're like a faulty tap—one moment cold, then hot, then back to cold again.' Horrified by the inexplicable torrent of words that seemed to be pouring from her of their own volition, she made a monumental effort to get a grip on herself. 'There's a first-aid kit in my office—perhaps there's some calamine lotion in it.'

A hand shot out, catching her by the arm as she turned to make her escape.

'How about if we both try keeping our cool . . . if we sit down and talk?' he suggested quietly.

Sian froze, her mind suddenly crystal clear. How could she possibly talk to him? The attraction she felt towards him both puzzled and frightened her—it could only be unnatural to feel such attraction towards a man she positively hated.

But her mind lost its clarity and became hazy again as she tried conjuring up those many reasons she had to hate him: the harsh anger he could inject into their everyday exchanges, the cold mockery that more often than not was in his eyes when they sought hers.

'What makes you think we have anything to talk about?' she asked stiltedly, while her mind perversely presented her with images of that handsome face softened by laughter, transformed by tenderness, of eyes darkened not in anger but with the stirrings of desire.

'Sian, don't let's pussyfoot around—we have a problem,' he snapped, picking up his shirt and easing his body into it.

'That problem being that you refuse to admit you took at face value what I was saying the day you arrived,'

accused Sian, launching into attack to distract herself from
the disturbing images still dancing in her mind.

'OK—it threw me,' he admitted reluctantly. 'But I
had no difficulty accepting it wasn't what it had seemed.'

'Really? You could have fooled me,' snapped Sian.

'Sian, please,' he sighed. 'Why don't you sit down?' He
moved round and sat at his desk, then began buttoning his
shirt. 'Didn't you learn *anything* about me the other night
. . . at Sir George's?' he asked quietly.

Because she had no intention of answering his question,
Sian busied herself by sitting down on the chair in front of
the deak.

'Because I learned quite a bit about you,' he continued,
tilting back in his chair and gazing up at the ceiling. 'It
must be pretty obvious to you that the last thing I'm
looking for is a relationship with a woman. Some wounds
take a long time to heal, and I wouldn't be able to guarantee
I'd be anything but bad news in any new relationship.'

Several thoughts were crossing Sian's mind as he spoke.
Such as why had she been so foolish as to sit down? And
why should he be discussing with her the whys and
wherefores of his future romantic liaisons?

'I'm meant to be your assistant, not some sort of tame
psychologist for you to vent your hang-ups on,' she
informed him tartly, rising as she spoke. This time there
was no way he was going to stop her leaving. 'You seem to
forget, I've already been subjected to the repercussions
of your confiding in me, and I've no intention of going
through it a second time.'

'My ears tell me it's English you're speaking,' he
drawled, rising also and walking round the desk to stand
a couple of paces from her. 'So how come I don't
understand a word of what you're saying?'

Sian took a hasty step backwards, cursing inwardly as the backs of her legs hit the chair from which she had just risen.

'Perhaps words of one syllable will help,' she snapped, furious with herself for the way she was having to scrabble backwards around the chair. 'You managed to sound almost human when you were telling me about Patty—a confidence you soon regretted and immediately began taking out on me in your usual charmless style!'

'You'd make a lousy psychologist, Sian. Your reasoning's way off,' he replied, then gave an exclamation of impatience. 'To hell with all this playing with words! As you've obviously gathered, I'm not the most altruistic of men, but, for both our sakes, I can't afford to let you get under my skin . . . Sian, right now—even if you were free—I don't need you or any other woman in my life.'

Not free, indeed! It was *his* damned rule about mixing business with pleasure, not hers!

'It may come as a shock to you, but I have no wish whatsoever to feature in your life!' she retaliated, pale with fury. 'That's the sort of thing you should try telling that battalion of women constantly ringing you here! I'd have some peace to get on with my work, instead of wasting my time dealing with their inane calls.'

'Do they bother you, Sian?' he asked mockingly, slowly advancing on her. 'Because they don't bother me any.' His hand streaked out and caught her by the wrist as she turned to make her escape. 'You're the only one who bothers me,' he murmured, tugging her against him. 'And you're a hypocrite if you refuse to admit the feeling's mutual.'

There was nothing even approaching gentleness in the mouth that took hers. And there was no element of caress in the hands that reached up to hold her head imprisoned, as those lips took their bruising possession of hers.

'Fighting me proves nothing,' he whispered against her mouth, as she fought to tear free.

It would prove something to her, thought Sian frantically as she tried to twist her mouth away from the disturbingly exciting onslaught of his. It would prove she at least had sufficient will power to resist this humiliating physical attraction he was capable of wielding over her.

Unclenching the hands that had been pummelling with no effect at his shoulders, she dropped them to his chest, slamming them against him and pushing with all her might.

The cry that escaped him had nothing to do with passion. It was a sharp groan of agony that pierced her senses, as his head dropped to her shoulder and his body slumped heavily against hers.

'Nick . . . I . . . oh, hell, are you all right?' she gasped, her arms automatically offering their support. 'I forgot all about . . .'

'My fault,' he groaned, his face pale as he lifted his head from her shoulder and gazed down at her. 'The only time in my life I've resorted to caveman tactics—and the lady practically KOs me!'

'Nick, I'm sorry, I honestly didn't mean——'

'For heaven's sake, what are you apologising for?' he protested hoarsely. 'I'm the one who should be down on his knees, begging you to——'

'There's no need to get carried away,' murmured Sian, trying desperately to inject some humour into her shaking voice, all the while wondering what it was about this man that he could move her in an instant from complete fury to this alien, almost maternal, confusion of anxiety.

'That's my problem, though,' he sighed, his hand reach-

ing out to smooth back the curtain of hair falling across her
face. 'With you I have a habit of getting carried away—to
places I've never been before.'

The soft caress of his words made Sian suddenly aware
that the arms she had reached out to support him were still
around him. Then there was a new awareness in her, of the
amount of time he was allowing her to step back from
him—to walk away—as his hand moved down, slipping
beneath her hair to caress in a tingling warmth at the back
of her neck.

She moved, not away, but tilted her head the fraction that
allowed her gaze to meet eyes that were almost navy in the
smouldering darkness of their blue.

'Sian, I'm sorry I . . . that I attacked you like that . . .
I . . .' With a soft groan he pulled her against him, his arms
enfolding her against him.

For an instant his mouth was a coaxing gentleness on
hers, probing, yet almost diffident, until the instant her
lips parted in unconscious acceptance. Then it was as
though a fast-burning fuse had reached its destination,
igniting in them both an explosion of need that became
a frantic probing of mouth against mouth, tongue against
tongue.

Her arms rose to cling round his neck, a soft moan
escaping her as sure hands swept up her body to cup the
straining fullness of her breasts beneath the soft material of
her blouse.

Her mind and body bombarded by sensations they had
never before experienced, she clung to him, her fingers
entwining and luxuriating in the glossy thickness of his
hair, while her body gave its melting, acquiescent response
to the harshness of desire in his. And there was no
reluctance in the totality of her response, no small voice

of sanity to censure her, for within her was the unquestionable knowledge that—no matter what conflict there had been, and might always be, between them—this inexplicable magic now possessing them was something that had caught them both in its spell.

'Sian, for heaven's sake, do something sensible—like getting out of here,' he groaned softly, his arms tightening fiercely to make it impossible for her to heed his plea, while his mouth began exploring her face, moving down her neck in a trail of softly tantalising kisses, till his tongue found and teased against the small pulse beating wildly at her throat.

The sound of the telephone on the desk beside them shattered through the silence, shrill in its harsh demand that they return to reality.

Nick's first reaction was an impatient shake of his head. Then he gave a softly groaned laugh of disbelief.

'So, that's what they mean by "saved by the bell",' he said, his voice breathless and unsteady.

He reached across and picked up the receiver, and Sian wondered what the person on the other end of the line had made of his hoarse, almost unrecognisable croak of his name.

And she was having difficulty recognising herself, she thought in stunned, churning bewilderment. It was as though she had become another person—a stranger she barely knew. She glanced up, the eyes of the stranger in her almost feasting on the strong, attractive features of the man now listening intently, a small frown creasing his brow.

She remained perfectly still as he listened, though her mind darted from one thought to the next, throwing out questions—such as why the fact that he kept one arm firmly around her shoulder should be bringing her such inordinate comfort—yet providing no answers.

'Will that create a difficulty?' he asked, his words sharp, though the lips that uttered them seemed fuller, softer in definition, to Sian's probing gaze.

Her gaze moved upwards, away from the disturbing sensations its inspection of his mouth was evoking, to his eyes—only to find them hooded from her sight. She examined the thick shadow of lashes fanning out darkly from his lids, and felt a new feeling pervading her, killing the churning excitement of arousal still lingering within her—and that feeling was an inexplicable, yet positive, fear.

'Listen, Alan, it's best if I come down,' he stated abruptly. 'Give me ten . . .' The dark fan of lashes lifted to reveal humour dancing among the dying embers of desire in the eyes that met Sian's. 'No, better make that five minutes.'

Had she not been so preoccupied by the fear, now firmly rooted within her, she might have found the decidedly passionless hug he gave her, after replacing the receiver, more than a little disconcerting.

'Perhaps I should have made that just one minute,' he murmured, his eyes twinkling as his hand reached out and softly stroked her cheek before he stepped away from her. 'Don't look so scared, Sian—we'll just have to work at it till we find the peaceful medium between us yelling at one another and behaving like kids just discovering what it is that makes the world go round.'

CHAPTER SEVEN

SIAN careered into the tall figure of her cousin as she entered the kitchen.

'It's about time you were up,' he teased. 'But I have to dash. Anna's salvaging your share of the masterpiece I've been slaving over a hot stove to create!'

'Oh, Toby, I'm sorry,' groaned Sian, glancing at her watch. 'But I'm not that late,' she protested as she saw the time.

'No—but I have to be early today. See you this evening!'

Sian winced as the door slammed behind him, then stepped into the kitchen. 'Morning, Anna. Why's Toby in such a rush?'

'The Collingwood trial starts today,' stated Anna, retrieving a plate from the warming-drawer and handing it to Sian with a grin.

'Oh, heck, I should have wished him luck!' Sian exclaimed, her eyes widening in alarm as she examined the contents of the plate. 'Anna, what on earth is this?'

'I think—though I'd not be prepared to swear to it— it's a Spanish omelette.' Anna chuckled. 'I didn't like to ask, especially when he seemed so proud of it—though I did manage to dissuade him from using the three cloves of garlic he'd painstakingly prepared to go in it!'

'Poor Toby.' Sian grinned. 'You realise this is all for your benefit—he's so overwhelmed by your fabulous cooking, he's attempting to repay you in kind!' She gave a small shudder as she glanced once more at the brightly coloured concoction on the plate. 'Anna, I honestly couldn't face this—not for breakfast,' she sighed. 'It's at times like this I really miss Mungo,' she added, feeling guilty as she scraped the contents of the plate into the waste disposal. 'He's a universal dustbin.' She glanced up and laughed as she caught sight of the puzzlement on Anna's face. 'My dog,' she explained, her expression softening wistfully. 'Well, technically he's mine, though he lives in Chiddingfold with Toby's parents. He's a Labrador; black, slightly overweight, very sloppy and completely adorable. Mind you, he's getting on a bit, he'll be fourteen next birthday, though you wouldn't believe it.'

'It's a shame you can't have him here,' murmured Anna, handing her a coffee. 'Though I suppose it wouldn't be fair on him.'

'Nor on my aunt and uncle,' Sian said with a chuckle. 'They'd never forgive me if I so much as suggested it— not that I would. Mungo's a country lad, he's not too keen on London.' She followed Anna to the table and took the seat beside her. 'Toby and I haven't been home for weeks now—how do you fancy a weekend in the country? You'd love my Aunt Evelyn and Uncle George, and you'd be able to meet Mungo in person!'

'It's very sweet of you to suggest it,' murmured Anna, gazing down into her coffee-cup. 'Sian . . .' She hesitated. 'Don't feel you have to include me in trips to your family, just because I lodge here.'

Sian glanced at her sharply, puzzled by something she found difficult to place in her tone.

'Anna, the fact that you live here has nothing to do with it—you're my friend,' she told her gently. Her face clouded as realisation began dawning on her. 'I know I've seemed to push you away recently when you've tried to ask me the sort of questions a friend is entitled to ask. Anna, I need your friendship, it means more than I can say to me, but I need time to . . . I suppose, to adjust to friendship—which must sound like gibberish to you,' she finished with a sigh.

'Almost,' murmured Anna, her smile wry before her face grew serious once more. 'Sian, all I ask is that you be completely honest with me about my living here. You would tell me if it wasn't working for you, wouldn't you? I'd understand.'

'Anna, whatever makes you ask that?' groaned Sian, horrified.

'It's just that for the past few weeks you've been so . . . so unhappy,' stated Anna miserably. 'I know how hard you've tried not to show it—but it does show, and I know it can't be work, because you and Nick are getting on so well now and——'

'Anna, please . . . stop!' begged Sian, a terrible guilt washing over her at the realisation of how her recent behaviour must have hurt this kind and gentle girl. 'Anna, if it's the last thing I ever do, I must explain, or attempt to explain, the way I am.' She broke off, wondering if she were capable of putting into words something she had only begun to come to terms with very recently. 'Apart from Toby and my uncle and aunt, I've had to make do without friends since . . . since I was very young.'

'Had to?' asked Anna, obviously perplexed.

'It seemed a necessity to me,' sighed Sian. 'The little I've already told you about myself is a hundred per cent more than I've ever told anyone else. The hang-up I had about something having happened to my aunt, when I was sent away to prep school, wasn't merely a hang-up—for a while I was so devastated by it, I cut myself off from all the other children. But one little girl eventually got through to me—Wendy—and we became the closest of friends.' She closed her eyes, the echo of that long-forgotten pain stirring once more in her. 'At the start of the second year, Wendy just didn't come back to school—her father, a diplomat, had been posted to Washington.'

The process that had turned a naturally gregarious child into a loner had been relatively swift.

'I was distraught without her to begin with, then all it took was a couple more such experiences for me to decide to cut my emotional losses.'

By the time she reached her teens, she had a wide circle of acquaintances—but she had long since forgone the painful luxury of close friendships.

'Anna, your friendship means so much to me—it only brings it home to me how inept I am at showing how I feel, if I've given you the impression I don't want you here.'

Anna reached over and patted her hand. 'I'm to blame, too—I've been so worried about you, I've been putting two and two together and coming up with five,' she murmured sheepishly. 'Just remember, though, if ever you need an ear—mine's available.' She glanced down at her watch and jumped up. 'We'd better get our skates on!'

They made their way to work, negotiating the rush-hour crowds in a silence that was purely companionable.

But Sian's thoughts were racing. She knew she had been withdrawing into herself during the past weeks, burying herself, whenever she could, in her work, taking manuscripts home in order to keep her mind occupied. She had felt small stabs of guilt on the occasions she had rebuffed Anna's tentative, and obviously caring, attempts to draw her out. But it had never once crossed her mind what interpretation Anna might put on her behaviour.

She had been so wrapped up in her own baffling state of mind, she had behaved with thoughtless selfishness towards someone who was incapable of selfishness, she thought guiltily.

'Anna,' she blurted out, goaded by remorse, 'have you ever had a problem you couldn't even try to explain to a friend, because you were incapable of explaining it to yourself?'

Anna shook her head, her expression sympathetic. 'I'd probably shove it to the back of my mind and pray that it went away.'

'I'll keep that in mind,' murmured Sian wryly, as they mounted the steps to the entrance. Suddenly she was brought to a halt by Anna's hand on her arm.

'I've just thought—I'm wasted in publishing,' exclaimed Anna, her expression dead-pan. 'I should set up as an agony aunt!'

There was a split second of silence, then the pair of them burst into gales of laughter.

They were still chuckling as they entered Sian's office.

'You know what I'm going to do?' announced Sian. 'I'm going to ring Toby and wish him luck—and thank him for a magnificent breakfast.' She paused, grinning as she shook her head. 'I'll have to word the breakfast bit diplomatically—I don't want him getting it into his head that it's normal to start the day on a Spanish omelette—if Spanish omelette is what it actually was,' she joked.

'Sian, could I see you for a moment—when you're ready?'

She glanced up, just in time to see the door of Nick's office closing behind him.

'I didn't realise he was there,' she muttered, slipping out of her coat, acutely conscious of the terrible dryness suddenly in her mouth.

'He's been quite an early bird of late,' called Anna from the door of her own office. 'I meant to tell you, I'll have to make do with grabbing a sandwich for lunch, I've a deadline to meet.'

Sian barely heard the words, she was too busy preparing herself to face Nick—something she had found herself confronted with every morning since the animosity between them had gone.

And each morning it was getting worse, she thought despondently, filling her with more dread than any she had felt during those weeks when they had been openly at loggerheads.

'. . . we'll just have to work at it till we find the peaceful medium between us yelling at one another and behaving like kids just discovering what it is that makes the world go round.'

She experienced again that strange fear which had filled her in the moments before he had spoken those words—a fear that had been almost a premonition, anticipating his words and warning her that, for them, there could be no happy medium.

If anything, she had coped better with his initial straightforward animosity than she was now with his relentlessly polite friendliness.

She hesitated beside her desk, knowing she should go in to him, yet held back by the thoughts now crowding into her mind.

It was with a sense of relief that she turned to the phone, which had just begun to ring—a welcome distraction—and lifted the receiver.

'Could I speak with Nicholas Sinclair, please?'

Here we go again, she thought, an expression of weary resignation flitting across her features. Though, to be fair, these calls from—she supposed—admiring women, had understandably tailed off recently with his refusal to accept all but a minuscule proportion of them. This voice, with its soft American tones, was one she didn't remember hearing before.

'I'm not sure if Mr Sinclair's in,' she lied, with the smoothness of practice. 'Who shall I say is calling if he is?'

'Patty Emmerson.'

The name was vaguely familiar, thought Sian—perhaps the woman had, after all, called before. She reached out to press the button of Nick's extension and suddenly her finger froze.

'I knew her as Patty Emmerson . . .'

So this was Patty, she thought, a peculiar churning sensation starting up in the pit of her stomach; the woman who, far more than Wally's death, had been the cause of Nick's leaving New York . . .

With an impatient toss of her head, Sian dismissed her thoughts—sympathy was one thing, but getting anxious on his behalf was overdoing it! She buzzed his extension.

'There's a Patty Emmerson on the line,' she announced, her tone giving no indication of her having recognised the name. 'Shall I put her through, or palm her off?' she added, using the now standard words that had become something of a joke between them.

Instead of eliciting his usual groaning chuckle, her words were met with a total silence.

Sian found herself trying to picture his expression. Surprise? Anger? Pleasure?

'Nick?'

'You'd better put her through.'

As she did as he asked, Sian found herself having to resist an almost overwhelming temptation to listen—just to his initial greeting. With an unnecessarily noisy clatter, she replaced the receiver.

She was bound to feel a certain sympathy for him, she reasoned, as her thoughts clung to the conversation now taking place. What were his feelings at this precise moment she wondered, as he spoke to the woman whose air of zany mystery had so attracted him . . . as he spoke to the woman he claimed only to have thought he loved, yet had contemplated marrying?

People didn't *think* they were in love, she reasoned—her eyes never once leaving the red engaged light on the telephone console—they were either in love or they were not.

It was several minutes before the light went out. About time too, thought Sian impatiently, rising and approaching the door of his office. She had been beginning to feel a bit of an idiot, sitting there waiting for the light to go out—but how else would she have known when he was free for her to go in?

'You wanted to see me?'

He had been sitting at his desk, so lost in his thoughts that he seemed not to have noticed her entering.

He glanced up, his features completely devoid of expression.

'Yes—sit down, Sian,' he muttered. 'There are a couple of things I need to discuss with you.'

Sian sat, her eyes curious as they looked him over.

No welcoming smile; no offer of coffee; none of the polite charm to which he had been subjecting her for several weeks now—that charm which had always stirred vague feelings of guilt in her, because deep down she was unable to shake off the conviction that he was studiously playing a role. And she couldn't put this change in him totally down to the call from Patty Emmerson, she realised suddenly, because his initial greeting this morning had been decidedly low-key by the standards set over recent weeks.

'. . . that Sir George will be spending some time up here with herself and Mike.'

'How is Sir George now?' asked Sian, wondering for how long her straying thoughts had blotted out his words, and praying she had missed nothing significant.

'Just dandy, according to Beverley. She says he's raring to get the contracts signed, so she and Mike have invited us to have dinner at their place on Friday—the contracts should be ready for us to take along. Will Friday be OK for you?'

'Yes, that'll be fine—I'm rather looking forward to seeing all three of them again,' murmured Sian. There could be no denying how the atmosphere between them had changed—and changed considerably. His manner was now so formal as to be bordering on cold.

'Good.' He flipped open the diary beside him on the desk. 'Next week I'll be away for a few days—in Ireland.'

'A holiday?' Sian's words were deliberately flippant, a conscious effort to lighten the atmosphere.

He shook his head, his non-committal expression an indication that he had no intention of responding. 'It's to do with the manuscript I brought over with me—there are a few points that need discussing with the author.'

'I'm glad things are getting moving on it. I loved it and Margaret thinks it's a winner—she's not often wrong,' said Sian, conscious of how stilted she was beginning to sound. 'I wonder why the author didn't use an Irish publisher—though I'm glad she didn't,' she added more easily.

He shrugged, his expression lacking interest. 'I don't think she had much idea what to do with it, so she sent it to her nephew, a friend of mine in New York—he passed it on to me.'

Her eyes firmly trained on her lap, Sian listened to his softly spoken words. He sounded almost preoccupied—she gave an imperceptible shake of her head as the sound of Patty Emmerson's voice seemed to ring in her ears. He had begun speaking again, his tone formal, meticulously polite, as he listed, then began expounding on, the items she would be attending to in his absence.

His instructions were detailed and precise, those of a man knowing exactly what was required in a job, the basics of which he had graspsed with a speed that had amazed her and had been greeted with heartfelt relief by the senior staff. Of course, he would never possess Simon's brilliant, almost intuitive flair, she reflected loyally, but there was no denying that only an exceptional mind could absorb and implement knowledge in the manner his had. Only recently she had learned he had also taken over much of the routine side of Wally's work.

'And now we come to this Joel Henderson hash-up,' he stated quietly, linking slim, brown fingers on the blotter before him and gazing candidly across at Sian.

Sian's eyes dropped from his, her blood chilling. The subject had never really come up since her chat with Margaret, and consequently it was something she had managed to put from her thoughts.

Unsure whether or not he was expecting her to say something, her eyes returned to his. Perhaps she was being over-sensitive, but she was positive she detected impatience beneath the surface of the enigmatic blue of his gaze—a look she had almost forgotten.

'I understood from you that all Simon entrusted to you was dealing with unsolicited manuscripts—and that only after you'd been here several months.' There was no accusation in his tone, he seemed merely to be stating facts.

'Well . . . yes,' she began, her mouth drying up on her—as was her brain, she realised with a stab of panic. She could not, for the life of her, recall precisely the alterations she had made to the files . . .

'Sian, I realise there's little to be gained in blaming you—you'd scarcely been here five minutes——' He broke off, his eyes coldly clinical as they regarded her. 'I suppose Margaret's already been over it all with you.'

'Over what?' croaked Sian, unsure whether he had been asking her a question or merely making a statement—probably because her mind had now seized up on her completely.

'Whether there could be paperwork around that you'd overlooked,' he snapped. 'Whether Simon may have had reason to use attorneys other than ours—hell, anything that could throw even a glimmer of light on what's gone on! You don't fight a lawsuit with faith; it takes solid facts.'

'I know that . . . but there's nothing I can think of . . . I'm sorry,' muttered Sian.

'She's sorry,' he drawled, his voice dripping sarcasm, as he flung himself back in his chair.

Her face tight with anger, Sian stood up. 'If that's all, I've work to be getting on with.'

'Did I say that was all?' he asked, open challenge in his eyes.

'Though it comes as something of a relief that you've finally dispensed with the taxing role of trying to be charming to me, I don't intend hanging around for this to deteriorate into a slanging match!' snapped Sian, turning on her heel and marching to the door.

That he reached the door before she did startled her

completely. Even a trained athlete, given his height and powerful build, would have been hard pressed to move as swiftly and silently as he had.

'You seem to be overlooking why I was being so painstakingly charming to you,' he taunted softly, lounging back against the door and blocking her exit.

'Painstaking being the operative word,' she retorted heatedly, unable to heed the inner voice warning her to stay calm at all costs.

'Don't remind me—come the end of most days, my jaw ached from all that smiling,' he declared, in tones more usually reserved for describing feats of heroism. 'But now all that's behind us, we come to the really interesting part,' he mocked, opening his arms as though inviting her to step into them.

'Would you mind getting out of my way?' asked Sian stiffly. 'As I said, I've work to do.'

'We've been through this routine before, Sian.' His tone had changed to the softness of seduction. 'And, in case you'd forgotten, it ends with you in my arms and the rest of the world on ice. So, what's it to be? Not that there really is any choice.' His hands reached out to her shoulders, their touch light, almost impersonal, as he teasingly shook her.

'Your idea of humour is about on a par with that of a ten-year-old schoolboy,' accused Sian scathingly, appalled by a terrible lack of faith in her own will to resist should he take her into his arms. The instant his hands had reached out to her, she had felt those alien, yet somehow familiar, sensations of melting and excitement stirring within her.

'No humour was intended,' he drawled, his eyes capturing hers in cool, glittering watchfulness. 'And my reasoning is purely adult. You've dismissed my attempts to be agreeably civil—can't say I have many regrets in that

department—but I have no yen to return to daily spats.'
The pressure of his hands increased a fraction on her
shoulders. 'So, all we have to fall back on is this very
intriguing physical effect we have on each other.'

'We obviously differ in our interpretation of the word
adult,' snapped Sian, angrily twisting free of his hold.

'How about coming into my arms and saying that?' he
taunted softly.

'If you want to play silly games, find someone else! Your
friend Patty, for instance!' She was regretting her words
even in the instant she was recklessly hurling them at
him. She had accused him of being juvenile, yet her own
words rang with the petty illogicality of a retaliating child.
'Please, Nick . . . just let me out of here,' she pleaded
wearily.

With a mocking bow, he stood aside and threw open the
door for her.

The fury on her face, as she marched past him, was
directed more at herself than at him. She *always* rose to
whatever bait he threw at her, she berated herself, and this
time she had paid by making a monumental fool of herself.
What on earth had possessed her to drag Patty into it? With
a shudder of disbelief, she turned as she reached her desk,
and immediately let out a yelp of surprise as she found
Nicholas Sinclair virtually on her heels.

'I hadn't finished talking to you,' he stated blandly.
'Perhaps you'd feel better if I told you what Patty had to
say——'

'No, I damn well wouldn't!' Sian almost shrieked, then
pulled herself up sharply and rephrased her words. 'I've no
interest whatsoever in what either of you has to say to the
other. Why should I? Nicholas, I have work to do!'

'Nicholas? Sian, is that an indication that you're mad

at me?' he asked innocently, a totally malevolent gleam in his eyes as he sat himself on her desk-top. 'Don't let me interfere with your work, but I just thought it might be wise to ask for your address now—in case we're not speaking come Friday.'

'For heaven's sake!' exclaimed Sian, angrily tugging open a drawer and removing a folder from it. 'You know my address.' She opened the folder, determined to ignore him.

'So, you're still there, are you?' he asked, his tone icy, his fingers flicking idly through the message-pad on her desk.

'I'm perfectly happy where I am. I've no idea what gave you the idea I might have moved,' she retorted, removing the message-pad from his reach and instantly regretting the action for its pettiness. Not even Toby, during their childhood years, had ever been able to reduce her to this infantile level, she thought resentfully, toying with the idea of moving into Anna's office, then immediately discarding it—he was perfectly capable of following her in there and continuing his inane, yet humiliatingly fruitful, baiting.

'I have what the realtors described as an eminently desirable residence——'

'The what?' exclaimed Sian, before she could stop herself, then mentally kicked herself for what was tantamount to encouraging him.

'Realtors—people who sell property. I can never remember what they're called here.'

'Estate agents—Nick, is there a point to any of this, or are you merely exercising your vocal cords?' asked Sian wearily.

'No, I'm not merely exercising my vocal cords,' he replied in a parody of an English accent.

Sian braced herself, expecting him to continue. After several seconds had passed, she glanced up to find him now engrossed in making a chain of her paper-clips. Later she would have the infuriating task of unlinking that lot, she thought irritably.

She was not going to utter a single word more to him, she vowed, her eyes firmly on the open folder before her.

'How about moving in with me, Sian?'

Sian's eyes remained locked on the now meaningless jumble of words before her. It was not just that his words had thrown her, which they had completely, but it was his dead-pan delivery of them that had her wondering whether her imagination hadn't suddenly run amok.

'Just you and me in an eminently desirable residence,' he coaxed, his soft words seeming to drip into her mind, wreaking havoc in it.

For no reason she could explain, her mind's eye began presenting her with images of the two of them, stepping through a large, brass-studded door. Then the door slammed behind them and Nick's arms were encircling her, and the thudding of her heart was a wild tattoo of excitement as his lips plundered hers.

'Either that, or you can help find me a housekeeper—I'm running low on shirts.'

CHAPTER EIGHT

'FOR pity's sake, you get on well with Beverley, don't you?' rasped Nick, slamming shut the passenger door after a tight-lipped Sian had seated herself in the car. 'Anyone would think you'd been left with your worst enemy, the way you're carrying on!' he continued once he too was in the car. 'Hell, Sian——'

'You understand perfectly well what I'm complaining about,' snapped Sian, wondering what on earth had possessed her to start this on leaving the Grades' home, reason niggling at the back of her mind and warning her she was being unreasonable. 'When you, Sir George and Mike disappeared—practically before the meal was over——'

'The meal *was* over, and you know damn well Sir George wanted to get the signing of the contracts over and done with. Hell, I had to insist on his reading them through——'

'And an hour later, when Beverley was forced to take coffee in to the three of you——'

'What do you mean—forced——?'

'The three of you were playing cards! If that isn't the height of bad manners . . . What the hell do you think you're doing?' she shrieked, as the seat in which she was sitting suddenly collapsed, carrying her startled body with it.

'I'm trying to get a word in edgeways, as they say,' grinned Nick, his hands lightly pinning her by the shoulders.

'Very funny,' glowered Sian. 'Let me up!'

'When I've had my say, you'll be allowed up—is that a deal?' he teased infuriatingly, leaning over her.

'Nick, if you don't let me up——' began Sian threateningly, then, realising she was hardly in a position to offer any threats, she scowled up at the laughing face above hers.

The drizzle which had greeted them as they had stepped out into the night now beat down on the car with an almost tropical intensity, distorting the light filtering through from the street-lamps till it rendered ghost-like and satanic the face peering down at her.

'If I don't let you up—you'll what?' he asked conversationally.

'Why don't you just say what you have to say?' suggested Sian, with as much dignity as she could muster, given the fact that she was trapped virtually flat on her back. 'It's obviously of earth-shattering importance, as you seem prepared to break every bone in my body to ensure——'

'Starting with your jaw.' He chuckled, releasing his hold on her shoulders. 'Sian, I didn't abandon you intentionally,' he added contritely.

'You know damn well that's not what I meant,' fumed Sian, her fingers searching to find the mechanism to return her flattened seat to the upright position.

'But after we'd finished with the contracts, Sir George produced the draft of something he's been working at on and off for years—a fascinating collection of freak bridge hands . . . Sian, what are you doing?' he asked, as her searching fingers grabbed at a knob and her seat lowered even further.

'I'm trying to raise the damned——'

'All this cursing you do—you realise it's the sign of a limited vocabulary?' he stated sanctimoniously. 'You're staying there till I've finished. Now, where was I? Ah, yes, Sir George's bridge hands . . . Mike and I, both being bridge-players, were naturally hooked the moment he dealt one of the hands——'

'Naturally,' muttered Sian sarcastically. 'While poor Beverley dithered around, wondering whether or not to serve coffee——'

'One thing Beverley *isn't* is a ditherer.' He chuckled, a throaty softness that danced beguilingly in the confined space. 'OK, so she ended up bringing the coffee in to us—but she was as pleased as punch to see my interest in her father's pet project——'

'You think it's worth publishing?' demanded Sian, her fingers toying with the lever once more—the seat couldn't possibly go any lower, she reasoned.

'I think so. I'll get Bill Gardiner to have a look at it; I hear he's a very keen bridge player.'

'I still think it was rude of you not to tell Beverley what you were doing immediately—after all, she was your hostess,' stated Sian primly, only to find an irritatingly rational voice within her pointing out that it was Beverley's father and husband, more than her guest, who deserved any blame.

Her eyes widened in alarm as Nick's face loomed over her—the dimness of the shadowed light making it impossible to discern his expression.

'It's at times like this I realise how lucky I am to have you,' he murmured, his tone verging on reverent.

Sian's eyes narrowed suspiciously, past experience warning her not to trust her ears.

'Shucks, honey, without you I'd never have known what a social embarrassment we hick Yankees can be to——'

'Very droll,' muttered Sian, unable to mask her amusement at his heavily parodied accent. 'Nick, please let me up . . .'

'You're staying put, I've not finished with you yet. Sian, I need to ask a favour.'

'Don't you think you should rephrase that?' demanded Sian, angry with herself for the way her guard was slipping. 'You intend barking another of your orders at me, more likely. Let me up!'

Without a word, he adjusted her seat—though still only raising it half-way.

'When have I ever barked an order at you?' he asked quietly.

He was serious, she thought, scarcely able to credit what she had heard.

'For heaven's sake, Nick, get on with it!' she exclaimed, her reaction hovering precariously between disbelief and the threat of laughter.

That was one of the things she found so infuriating about him, she told herself exasperatedly, the speed and ease with which he had her feeling as though she were on a mental see-saw.

'I can't go to Ireland next week—I want you to go in my place.'

'Fine—I'll go. Now I'd be grateful if you would take me home.'

There was an instant of silence after her coolly delivered words, then he threw back his head and laughed.

Sian turned slightly, glowering up at him through narrowed eyes as she fought the infection of his laughter—not that there was anything remotely funny about what she had said.

'OK, I'll take you home,' he managed eventually. 'But first, let's get you safely strapped in.' He leaned across to her seat-belt. 'No, perhaps the first thing is to get you upright,' he murmured.

Sian eased her body slightly as he reached for the lever; the next thing she knew, she was thrown even further backwards, and he was half-sprawled across her.

'You're practically suffocating me now,' she complained, her voice breathless and distorted.

She remained stock-still, inordinately conscious of his nearness as he repositioned her seat—a nearness that had not altered a fraction once he had finished the adjustment.

'Nick?' The tentative breathlessness in her call of his name startled her—her intention had been to convey indignation, impatience . . .

'I know,' he sighed, his hands gently cupping her face. 'I was a fool to come within a foot of you—if I'd had any sense I'd have told you to find your own way home.'

'In the pouring rain?' she queried, discovering she had no control over her strangely distorted speech.

'In the pouring rain,' he echoed softly, his head lowering till the tip of his nose was against hers.

Not moving a muscle, Sian closed her eyes. She had to, she rationalised, to stop them crossing.

'Sian, be honest—you haven't enjoyed the past few weeks any more than I have.' As he spoke those husky, almost seductive, words, his head moved gently from side to side, his nose rubbing lightly against hers.

'I've hated it,' agreed Sian miserably, and was immediately uncertain whether her misery was occasioned by the memory of the past weeks—or the naïveté of her spontaneous admission.

'Who'd be an Eskimo,' he whispered, 'if this is their substitute for kissing?'

It threw her how familiar the sensation of his mouth

seemed on hers, as his lips parted hers in a softly sensual search; how her mouth needed no guidance from his to know the sharp hunger of desire.

And there was that same hunger in her hands as they searched beneath the bulk of his coat and jacket till they found the vibrant warmth of him beneath them.

'But you know that kissing can only be the beginning of what I want from you,' he groaned softly, his hands warm against her flesh as they slid beneath the soft wool of her top. 'And that's why we have to stop this right now,' he protested hoarsely, his hands denying his words as they rose to cup her breasts.

Her answer was a soft, incoherent moan as his fingers began playing tantalisingly against the excited tautness of her flesh.

'Sian,' he whispered, a sudden urgency in his voice as he drew her closer to him, 'tell me you don't want me to stop!'

'Would you believe me if I said I did?' she whispered raggedly, her arms dragging free of the confines of his clothing to cling round his neck.

'No,' he groaned, his mouth hot in its passionate demand as it reclaimed hers. 'But something tells me thirty-one's a mite old to be carrying on like this in a car,' he protested, raining impassioned, random kisses around the vicinity of her mouth.

'Carrying on like what?' murmured Sian distractedly, her mind closed to all save the dizzying welter of excitement and sensation that was being in his arms.

He gave a soft, groaned laugh, his head dropping to the curve of her neck, where his lips began teasing against the erratic throb of the small pulse fluttering at her throat.

She buried her face in the silky thickness of his hair, her senses filled with the helpless intoxication with which her body seemed to respond automatically at his touch, her mind colluding with her body in its acceptance that this was a moment she wanted only to prolong.

'Sian, do me a favour and count to three,' he murmured huskily, his breath warm against her skin, before he drew away to gaze down at her.

'One, two, three,' she chanted in rapid succession, her arms meeting resistance as they tried to draw his head back to her.

'Slower,' he chuckled in protest, reaching up and catching her wrists.

'Why?' she demanded, alarm mingling with the excitement melting through her, as she became conscious of determination piercing the sultry message of desire in the darkness of his eyes.

'Because I have to do something to break this spell—if only temporarily.'

He brought her hands down from around his neck, creating a barrier between them as he imprisoned them against his chest.

'Sian, there's no way we can continue like this here.' His head dropped, his lips brushing against her imprisoned fingers before he lifted it again. 'Though where we go from here is up to you—whether to my place, where we really begin breaking all the rules, or——'

'Rules?' she whispered, the hint of censure in his words penetrating the strange euphoria possessing her. 'Why do you always speak of rules?'

Even as she spoke he was leaving her, taking with him the magic that had held her in its thrall, as he leaned back against his seat.

'Just let's say I'd have problems with my conscience if I were to spend the coming weekend as I'd like—making love to you,' he stated quietly, words that chilled her to the marrow with their unspoken message.

'I suggest you take me home—to my home,' she retorted through numbed lips. 'I've no intention of coming between you and your conscience.'

There was no point denying what would have happened had she gone with him to his home, she thought with complete detachment, and it was a thought that left her curiously free of any sense of humiliation.

'Sian, are you being deliberately obtuse?' he rasped, injecting an impression of fury into the way he gunned the powerful car to life.

'Why obtuse?' she retaliated, wishing she had kept her mouth shut, but, having opened it, feeling obliged to continue. 'It's not as though I've made any coy denials about the effect you have—we have on each other.' And it was because that effect was so completely mutual in its blatant need, she realised suddenly, that she had felt no humiliation. 'Just because I find a fact unpalatable doesn't mean I'd be stupid enough to deny it!' She gave a deep inward groan as the words slipped from her—why, for once in her life, could she not leave well alone?

'Admitting to the obvious doesn't alter the fact that you're being downright obtuse!' he snarled, flinging the car to a halt outside the flats and clipping the wing-mirror of Toby's immaculate BMW as he passed it.

Sian leapt out of the car, racing to the BMW and minutely inspecting it.

'Anyone would think I'd slammed into it, the way you're carrying on!' exclaimed Nick, as he reached her side. 'Don't people around here have garages?'

'He only left it out because we're driving down to Chiddingfold in the morning,' retorted Sian, relieved to find the mirror undamaged as she righted it. 'He was hardly likely to foresee you would be haring around here like a lunatic!' she accused.

'More fool him,' retorted Nick dismissively, his eyes narrowing as they flickered over her. 'What would you have done about your trip to the country had we ended up at my place?'

'In case you hadn't noticed, we didn't end up at your place!' Sian felt her blood boil as she remembered his reference to his conscience. She had heard of the term "one-night stand"—perhaps there was such a thing as a one-weekend stand . . . and that was all it would have been to him, had she given in to what now seemed like the madness that had possessed her. 'And there was never the remotest likelihood of our going to your place,' she declared coldly, resolutely ignoring the small voice within her that branded her a liar.

'You wouldn't care to put that to the test, would you?' he asked with soft venom, anger glittering in his eyes.

For a reason she could not fathom, Sian found her eyes drawn to the harsh line of his mouth. There had been the voluptuous softness of seduction in that same mouth when it had whispered against hers, and the memory shivered through her, sharp and savage in its sudden urgency.

'Unfortunately, I haven't the time to indulge in your childish games,' she managed eventually, unnerved to find none of the scathing dismissal she had intended discernible in her tone. 'I have to be up early in the morning . . . as you may have gathered.'

'As I most certainly have gathered,' he responded, with a small, mocking bow. 'Have yourself a great weekend.'

CHAPTER NINE

'HELLO Margaret?' Sian leaned back in the deep armchair, the telephone receiver cradled to her ear. 'I was hoping to have a word with Nick, but they tell me he's not in.'

'I'm afraid I've no idea of his movements today, my dear. I've only just got back into the office myself. 'How's Ireland?'

'Quite incredibly beautiful, but very stormy—I've been trying to get through since this morning. I believe the storms have brought down a few lines.'

'We're being blown all over the place here,' said Margaret. 'But I'm sure you weren't ringing for a weather report . . . how did things go with Eithne Jennings?'

Sian pulled a small face, giving silent thanks for Margaret's habit of coming straight to the point, and filled with inordinate relief that circumstances decreed it was she, instead of Nick, to whom she was now reporting.

'I'm not sure . . . I know that sounds silly,' she sighed, her mind still puzzling over her encounter with the Irish writer. 'I don't know if I've offended her, or what——I went to see her the day I arrived and went through all the points as briefed.'

'And?' coaxed Margaret as Sian hesitated.

'Perhaps I didn't explain as well as I should have—she unnerved me by not making a single comment. I felt a little as though I were delivering a sermon to a stony-faced congregation.'

'I don't see how anyone could possibly take offence

at having the routine requirements of a publishing house pointed out to her.' Margaret chuckled, her laughter a balm to Sian's ears.

'She didn't *seem* to take offence,' explained Sian. 'All she did, when I'd finished, was nod and say she didn't feel like dealing with it just then.'

Margaret gave an exclamation of impatience. 'I can't honestly see why Nick didn't simply write to the woman once he couldn't go, instead of sending you over there. I know we could well have a best-seller on our hands, but . . .'

'I think it's because it was a friend of his who gave him her manuscript—her nephew,' stated Sian, anxiety creeping into her tone. 'Though substituting me for Nick obviously wasn't such a good idea.'

'Sian, what exactly happened—after she said she didn't feel like discussing it then and there?'

'She offered to show me around——I didn't mean to give the impression she was unpleasant or anything; in fact, she was most charming. We went for a long walk, all round the village and for miles along the sands——'

'You obviously arranged to see her again . . .'

'Not exactly—she said she'd contact me. I didn't hear from her at all yesterday, then this morning her housekeeper arrived at the hotel with a note from her. It was to say she'd gone to Dublin—in fact, she left yesterday—and that she'd see me when she got back.'

'I can't see any problem in that. You'll just have to sit tight till she gets back,' observed Margaret, unperturbed. 'And for heaven's sake, stop being such a little worrier,' she added lightly. 'Spare a thought for us in dreary old London while you're relaxing in the Irish countryside—I hear the hotel you're in is very good.'

'It's beautiful,' agreed Sian. 'Definitely five-star-plus, even though they only have a skeleton staff in the winter. I'm the only guest and they've given me an entire suite of rooms; it's the only part of the hotel kept open at this time of year.'

'So put your feet up and enjoy it—and pray a winter coach-load doesn't arrive,' teased Margaret. 'Anyway, I'll get Nick to ring you——'

'No, there's no need to do that,' cut in Sian. 'I mean, I've told you all I'd have said to him. Margaret, could you have me transferred to Anna? I need——'

'Oh, dear, you're not having much luck with this call,' came Margaret's laughing interruption. 'Anna's not in this afternoon, either. If you have problems getting through to her from there, I'll get her to give you a ring in the morning.'

Sian said her goodbyes, a small frown creasing her brow as she replaced the receiver. She would have given anything for an opportunity to speak to Anna, she thought, with a sharp pang of guilt. She needed to clear the air with her—and with Toby too, for that matter.

She leaned back her head, her eyes closed and a tense, unhappy expression on her face.

She had behaved appallingly during the weekend in Chiddingfold, she reminded herself miserably, taking off for hours at a stretch, with Mungo faithfully at her heels, and barely exchanging a word with Toby and Anna. Thank heaven her uncle and aunt had taken so strongly to Anna, she thought, huge waves of guilt washing over her as she remembered Anna's uncharacteristic nervousness at the prospect of the weekend and the complete lack of support she had been given. Not that Toby had been much help, she reflected, remembering her cousin's unusual taciturnity, which had come close to matching her own. No, she was being unfair, Toby had merely seemed uncharacteristically down, whereas she . . .

With an exclamation of impatience, she leapt to her feet. If anyone were to be blamed, it was Nicholas Sinclair!

There was taut anger on her face as she marched to one of the tall windows in the spacious sitting-room that was part of the suite she now occupied. The anger seeped through her entire being as her mind became filled with that strong, masculine face which, in the past few days, seemed to have taken up more or less permanent residence in her thoughts.

She was obsessed with the wretched man! It was thanks to him she was on such tenterhooks that she was unable to be civil to her own family—to Anna; thanks to him that the sudden departure of Eithne Jennings had filled her with such self-recriminating doubts—the woman had probably planned her trip ages ago and merely forgotten to mention it!

She gazed through the rain-blurred windows, down past terraced lawns flanked by clusters of rhododendron bushes, and down further still to the white-flecked grey of the storm-tossed sea.

It *was* an obsession, she admitted miserably, a weird obsession in that it was so totally out of character, so utterly inexplicable. Yet there had to be a reason! Perhaps there was an element of vanity in it, a perverse attraction brought on by his cavalier treatment of her. She was used to being flattered—cosseted, even—by men. Even Roy, despite his criminal actions, had always treated her with kid gloves in their personal relationship—whereas the treatment meted out to her by Nick could only be described as the bare-knuckled variety.

She lowered her forehead to the sharp coldness of the

glass as the heat of remembered excitement flared in her. Or perhaps it was his physical effect on her that kept him so constantly in her thoughts. It was disconcerting, to say the least, to discover she was capable of physical longings over which she appeared to have virtually no control. Disconcerting, not so much because of the devastating strength of those hitherto unsuspected longings, but because they were triggered by a man with whom she had a relationship based solely on mutual antagonism.

She straightened, determination strengthening in her. If anything, she should be thanking her lucky stars for these few days alone, she told herself, her step firm as she returned to where she had been sitting. For the first time in days—perhaps weeks—she was thinking clearly.

She reached for the telephone, her sudden clarity of mind pin-pointing her priority—Anna.

'You're going to hate me,' she apologised to the receptionist. 'I'd like to place another call to London.' She found herself crossing her fingers as she gave the number.

'I'll do my best,' promised the girl, laughter in her friendly voice. 'But at least you'll have a bit of company if the wait for this one is as long as the last—Liam's on his way up now.'

There was puzzled amusement on Sian's face as she replaced the receiver. Was the loquacious Liam worried that she might be feeling lonely? It was he who had greeted her on her arrival—a jovial, balding and ruddy-cheeked character of indeterminate age—somewhere between fifty-five and seventy was all she had been able to estimate, as she had listened spellbound to his humorous potted history of his family and the magnificent Mullan Fort Hotel to which he welcomed her.

She had learned with an element of surprise that Liam

was a co-owner of the hotel with his brother—there was a cosy vagueness about him that made him seem somewhat at odds with the grandeur of his surroundings. Her surprise was borne out when he informed her it was only during the winter months, when his brother and sister-in-law took off to warmer climes and the hotel was virtually empty, that he was called on to do his bit towards the family business.

She was smiling broadly as she rose to answer the brisk rap on the outer door of the suite. A chat with Liam would cheer her up—if anyone had kissed the Blarney Stone it was he—and he might also be able to shed some light on Eithne Jennings' disappearance to Dublin.

'Just the man——' Her smile, the words of welcome, froze on her lips as she found herself gazing through the open door, past the beaming Irishman, at the tall, familiar figure to the back of him. 'What on earth are you doing here?' she gasped, a sudden pounding starting up in her ears, while her entire system seemed to run out of control.

'Could you not give the man a better welcome than that?' chided Liam, ambling past her, towards the door of the second bedroom. 'You'll be good and comfortable in here—it has a grand big bed in it,' he called over his shoulder to Nick, then entered the room without waiting for any reply.

'Why are you here?' repeated Sian, trying to inject a semblance of welcome into her tone as Nick stepped through the outer doorway, a leather holdall in his hand.

'You appear somewhat underwhelmed to see me, Sian,' he drawled, his glance barely taking her in as it flew to the door through which Liam had disappeared. 'Mr Kelly,' he called, depositing the holdall at his feet, 'I'd prefer a suite of rooms of my own, if you don't mind—or just a room will do.'

'The name's Liam,' announced the Irishman, appearing once more at the door. 'And this is a grand room . . .' He hesitated, smiling as the American's implacable expression suddenly registered. 'We just keep the one suite open in the winter,' he explained. 'Though there's never much call for it.' His glance moved to Sian, his eyes twinkling mischievously as he gave her a broad wink. 'There's a sturdy lock on the door, if you're worried about young Sian's intentions!'

Battling with the riot of emotions assailing her, and certain she was blushing to her roots, Sian waited for the explosion from Nick as she saw the ominous tightening of his jaw.

The explosion came—a softly rumbling outburst of laughter, before he picked up his bag and followed Liam into the room.

For several seconds she remained rooted where she stood, the sound of the voices emanating from the bedroom no more than a soft blur against her ears. Then she slowly returned to the sitting-room. Her faltering steps led her first to the window, through which she gazed sightlessly for mere seconds, then back to the small sofa, on which she had barely seated herself before she leapt once more to her feet to return to the window.

Her stomach was churning, she was shaking like a leaf and altogether she was behaving like a complete fool, she berated herself. Just as she was beginning to get herself sorted out—he had to turn up! Under the circumstances, her present over-reaction was perfectly understandable. But what the hell was he doing here?

She called out in reply to Liam's cheery farewell, every muscle in her body tensing as she heard Nick enter the room. She had already asked him twice why he was here, she thought mutinously, and she certainly wasn't going to ask a third time.

'If you've come to see Miss Jennings, she's in Dublin.'

'So I hear,' came the steely-toned reply. 'And I'm here to find out what it is you could have said to her to send her scurrying off like that.'

'What I said?' gasped Sian, spinning round in indignation. 'No wonder you gave up practising law, if you hold the belief a suspect is guilty until proved inno——'

'Can the wit, will you, Sian?' he drawled, flinging his long, lithe frame on to the small sofa. 'I called her yesterday morning because I needed to——'

'Because you needed to check up on your incompetent assistant,' flared Sian. 'I don't know what possessed you to trust me to come here in the first place!'

'Neither do I,' he retorted. 'Anyway, I got through to her housekeeper, who informed me Miss Jennings was very upset and had gone to Dublin. I spent the next several hours trying to call you here, but——'

'The recent storms have affected the lines,' she informed him, her tone cool despite the fact that her blood was boiling.

'As you still hadn't returned to London this morning, I decided the only thing to do was come over and find out what in hell's been going on.' There was undisguised censure in the eyes that flickered coldly over her.

'I'll tell you what the hell went on—I briefed her as I was instructed, word for word! Even I am capable of handling something as routine as that, believe it or not, though you——'

'Sian, I . . . oh, hell!' he exclaimed as the phone began ringing. 'I suggest you answer it,' he snapped, as Sian remained immobile by the window. 'As they won't have the message I'm here till tomorrow, it's unlikely to be for me.'

As she stirred herself, Sian was praying the receptionist had been unable to get through to Anna. The last thing she wanted—or would be capable of—was to make her peace with her friend in the presence of this glowering witness.

'Toby? I didn't expect you to be around——'

'Anna and I have been trying to get through to you all afternoon,' interrupted Toby, an unfamiliar edge to his voice.

'I've been having problems from this end, too . . . Toby, why the sudden need to speak to me?' she asked, an unaccountable apprehension colouring her tone.

'It's nothing urgent, love . . . it's . . . Sian, this is one of those times when I could ask if you wanted the good or the bad news first, but I don't want to sound flippant——'

'Toby, just tell me,' she urged quietly, her blood suddenly running cold.

'It's Mungo, love. He died last night—completely painlessly in his sleep . . . the vet told Dad that the old ticker just packed up on him.'

As she heard her cousin's words, Sian's mind became filled with vivid images from her childhood—of a black, almost fluffy bundle that had grown to become her adored and adoring companion.

'Sian?'

'Yes . . . I . . . I suppose I can only be glad it happened like that.' She had a vague impression of movement on the sofa across from her. Through eyes now blurring with tears, she glimpsed the puzzled anxiety on Nick's features and quickly turned away.

'There actually is some good news,' Toby was telling her gently. 'I hope it will ease things a little. Sian, one of the reasons this weekend was so——'

'Toby, I know I'm to blame for that, I was ghastly——'

'But it must have occured to you that normally I'd have pulverised you verbally,' butted in Toby, a surprising hint of laughter in his voice. 'Perhaps you didn't help, but the blame was mostly mine. I was waging a ridiculous battle with the inevitable, and making those I love suffer in the process—especially Anna.'

'Anna?' parroted Sian, almost immediately giving a silent groan as she remembered the numerous puzzling instances of late which she, in her selfish preoccupation, had chosen to ignore.

'You've been a mite preoccupied of late,' said Toby, almost as though reading her now guilt-racked mind. 'Otherwise you'd have noticed a bit of heart-swapping going on—not that I could fathom out what was happening, nor Anna, for that matter . . . I'd no idea it could happen so quickly!'

'Toby, are you saying that you and Anna . . .?' Her words choked to a halt and, through the tears now streaming down her cheeks, she scarcely noticed the tall figure rise from the sofa and leave the room.

'Sian, are you blubbering?' demanded Toby, chuckling.

'Of course I am! Oh, this is wonderful—I can't believe it! Is Anna with you?'

'Tucked under my arm and with an ear plastered to the phone,' he laughed. 'And you'll be pleased to hear that she's forgiven me for my initial boorish reaction to becoming inescapably hooked, and has agreed to marry me!'

While she and Anna had a tearfully incoherent exchange, Sian could hear Toby's teasing comments in the background. When she eventually replaced the receiver, she sat down, hugging herself with delight. It was only after

several minutes of basking in pleasure that her happiness
was nuzzled aside by memories of a cold, wet nose, and the
tears that welled once more in her eyes were no longer those
of happiness, but of an aching sense of loss.

'Sian . . . if I can help in any way . . .'

She started at the sound of that softly tentative voice, her
fingers scrubbing self-consciously at her cheeks as her gaze
met that of the man now standing in the doorway.

'Good news sometimes affects me like this,' she
announced defensively—there was no way she intended
leaving herself open to the sarcastic comments she felt him
quite capable of making had he known the reason for her
tears. 'I've just learned that two people I love very much
intend to marry,' she added, forcing brightness into her
voice.

'Sian, I . . . I'd no right to imply you were at fault over
Eithne Jennings,' he stated, the uncharacteristic hesitancy
still in his tone throwing her almost as much as his sudden
switch of subject. 'Now that I think of it, the friend who
gave me the manuscript did warn me she could be a bit
eccentric at times.'

'Actually, she was very nice,' said Sian, her words stiff
and formal. She managed to relax a little as she told him of
the woman's friendliness as she had shown her around. 'But
I have to admit it worried me—her just taking off . . .'

'I don't want you worrying about it,' he chided, startling
her by sitting on the arm of her chair and smiling down at
her. 'I'd probably have upset her by trying to push the
issue, so it's just as well I was tied up following what might
prove a very promising lead on the Henderson problem.'

Though it was a subject that still had the power to make
her feel slightly uncomfortable, Sian would have given
anything to have learned more—had it not been for a

more immediate consideration suddenly preoccupying her. Nick had leaned slightly closer, stretching one arm along the back of the chair, and with his free hand had begun lifting the strands of hair which had fallen across her face, returning them one by one to order. His movements were light, almost imperceptible, each one a hovering, weightless caress against her head.

'The lady is due back tomorrow and, until we've seen her, the subject is out of bounds—OK'

Sian's eyes remained as though transfixed on the dark material of his jacket filling her line of vision, while her mind raced into overdrive.

'OK,' she managed, barely audible.

'Sian, if we put our minds to it, we *could* be friends, despite our lousy track record.' He continued speaking, his words soft and conciliatory as he spoke of trying to put the past behind them. Then he was describing his reactions to the peaceful beauty of their surroundings, his words almost duplicating those that had sprung to her own mind when she had first arrived.

As he spoke, she had no need to see his face to know what was reflected in it—that face which, almost from the start, seemed to have engraved itself on her mind, conjuring its way into her thoughts at will, whether in anger or in laughter, in cool disdain or in passion. And now her mind's eye was showing her the teasing tenderness on that handsome face as he offered her his friendship—the friendship her heart so violently rejected, as recognition of love became a silent explosion of understanding within her.

It was his love she wanted, because it was love she had given him—no, not given—he had taken the love from her, had sneaked into her heart and stolen it, the last thing she had wanted to lose.

'Don't frown, Sian . . . please, don't be sad,' he coaxed softly, rising and taking her by the hand, bringing her upright and into the circle of his arms.

'I'm not sad,' she lied, every fibre in her recoiling from the unquestionably fraternal bear-hug in which he enveloped her before releasing her.

'OK, you're not sad,' he murmured, no rancour in the softness of his tone. 'So how about giving me a guided tour of this place? Take me where our absconded author took you . . . show me around all this beauty.'

'In this rain?' she asked, a dazed softness in her words, as her mind grappled with the question of how something now so stunningly obvious could have eluded her for so long . . . for how long? Probably from the first time she had tasted the joy of sharing his laughter, and known the dizzy intoxication of being held in his arms, she thought with bewilderment.

'Don't tell me you would turn chicken over a few lousy drops of rain?' he teased, something in his eyes sending the rhythm of her heartbeat lurching out of control.

As they retraced their footsteps along the sands a couple of hours later, with the wind-borne rain lashing in their faces, it occurred to her that a more realistic term for the volume of rain hurling down on them would be deluge. Not that such details had the power to hold her for any length of time, as her mind remained firmly trapped in the bewildering magic of loving. As though newly opened, her eyes were drinking in every minute detail of him as his tall figure turned, a few yards ahead of her, and faced her. There was laughter on his face as he began walking backwards, calling out words to her that had no chance of reaching her, as the gusting wind whipped them away and danced them out to sea.

How could she not have recognised the sheer inevitability of loving him? She, who had once so smugly believed that love would come neatly packaged and instantly recognisable, had lost her heart irrevocably to a man who fitted no recognisable mould—an urbane sophisticate with a beguilingly off-beat sense of humour, a man who could revel so wholeheartedly in the desolate beauty of their surroundings and laugh in joyous defiance of the torrenting heavens.

He stopped, waiting for her to catch up with him, and as she walked towards him the coldness of the rain on her face seemed to wash into her being, bringing with it a sharp flash of memory. It was the memory of the time she had stood beside him in his office, his arm encircling her as he spoke into the phone. And she was remembering the passion that had erupted between them, the reluctance with which they had parted with the sudden ringing of the phone. But most of all she was remembering the inexplicable fear that had taken hold of her as she had gazed up at him from within the sanctuary of his arm . . . a fear she had neither understood nor heeded then, but which was now no longer inexplicable. From somewhere, buried in her subconscious, that fear had sprung, warning her of the folly of what was probably happening to her even then—the folly of loving a man who had quite candidly told her that the last thing he needed in his life was her, or any other woman.

'You look cold,' he told her, not even the trace of recent laughter remaining on his face, as shrewd blue eyes swept over her. 'We'd best get you back to the hotel and into a hot tub.'

She nodded, the thoughtless happiness that had so briefly

possessed her now replaced by the cold chill of fear.

It was an all-pervading chill that had clung tenaciously throughout the evening. She had still been conscious of its presence even when, to her relief, Liam had joined them for their evening meal. And now, as the jovial Irishman bade them goodnight, casting her yet another of the puzzled glances he had given her throughout the evening, she felt it surge within her, expanding into a feeling that was almost panic.

In silence, she followed Nick up the staircase, conscious of the tautness of anger in him and knowing she had probably only seconds in which to offer an explanation before that repressed anger erupted from him.

She knew it had only been courtesy towards Liam that had held him in check throughout the evening. She had seen the suppressed anger in his eyes, as time and again she'd drifted and become lost in the turmoil of her own thoughts, completely losing the thread of any conversation and finding it impossible to participate even at so undemanding a level. If she were honest, she was surprised how long his patience had lasted before eventually snapping, and snap it undoubtedly had, even though Liam would have been completely unaware of that fact.

Her mouth dry with apprehension, she followed him into the dimly lit hallway of the suite, quietly closing the door behind them. He stopped so suddenly, she almost collided with him, and she felt herself visibly recoil from the saturnine harshness of his features, immobile save for the one tell-tale muscle working at the hollow of his left cheek.

'Nick, I . . . I don't know what came over me. I . . .' With a hopeless shrug, she reached out a hand to him, a gesture that was part reflex, part a plea for forgiveness.

'Sian, my anger wasn't directed at you . . .' As he spoke,

his hand reached out and met hers.

In that one instant their hands met, in the next they were locked in an embrace of almost savage intensity, their lips clinging in a bruising, searching hunger that contact seemed unable to assuage.

'Why do you always assume my anger is directed at you?' he groaned, his lips barely letting up in their frantic plunder of hers. 'Sian, I can't reason when I'm holding you, but you must know that friendship isn't the word for what you'll find in my arms——'

'I know,' she whispered, her words cutting across the hoarse outpouring of his. 'I know,' she repeated, almost as though comforting him.

'The physical effect you and I have on each other makes rational thought impossible at times like this, but later . . . later there could be regrets.'

She buried her face against him, her arms clinging in desperation, her head shaking in denial. What possible regrets could she ever feel for giving physical expression to the love that was already his? Whatever his arms offered her, in hers he would find only love.

'I'll have no regrets,' she promised softly, her words a commitment to love. 'I know what I'm doing.'

'But do I know what I'm doing.' he groaned, his mouth opening on hers in a kiss that seemed to search into her soul. 'Oh, Sian, how I want you! Don't run away from me this time . . . I can't let you go!' The same restless urgency that was in his words was in the hands that swept over the contours of her body, drawing her ever closer to him and filling her with an intoxicating need so powerful that it drove a shuddering cry of longing from her.

'Don't let me go,' she begged, the words spilling from her unrecognised, as the restlessness of his searching hands gained purpose, gentling against her as he unbuttoned her dress, sliding it from her shoulders to let it fall at her feet.

Then those hands were sending violent shock-waves of sensation coursing through her; delicately sensuous fingers were moving in seductive play against her flesh as they deftly removed the lacy wisps of her underwear. There was nothing she could do to silence the soft, incoherent cries of his name that poured from her in a wild, sobbing chant, and there was nothing she could do to control the savage power of the need surging through her, racking her body in shivering tremors as her mind retreated to the periphery of awareness.

When he lifted her, swinging her up into his arms, and began carrying her, she was lost in the message of the mouth that remained locked with hers, answering its questing, impassioned demands with searing demands of her own. And when he lowered her on to the bed she clung to him, her only thought to keep him in her arms as she felt him move to break free.

'If you won't let me go, you'll have to undress me,' he protested huskily.

'I won't let you go,' she whispered, her trembling fingers fumbling against the buttons of his shirt.

The soft rumble of his laughter sent a shiver of excitement coursing through her, and it was only when his laughter once again caressed her ears, as he chided her lack of dexterity, that her mind momentarily awoke to the blatancy of her actions. But that moment was forgotten the instant he drew her into his arms, and the cry that spilled from her was one of shock and pleasure as, for the first time in her life, her body felt the raw, sensuous power of a naked male body against it. There was no fear in her, only exultation as her body moved in melting wonderment against his, revelling in the sharp, quivering need that rippled through the length of him, as her trembling hands began imitating the tingling web of ecstasy his were tracing against her burning skin.

Then her cry was one of pleading as he buried his head in the desire-tautened swell of her breasts, the touch of his lips and the sharp caress of his teeth filling her with such a torment of need that pleasure became a time-bomb, ticking away within her till an inevitable moment of explosion.

'Sian, you're trembling,' he whispered huskily, breaking free from the frantic restrictions of her arms to gaze down at her in the paleness of moonlight softening the room. 'You're not afraid?'

'I'm not afraid,' she choked, her fingers reaching up to trace the outline of his beloved face. 'But I can't stop shaking . . . Nick, I——' She broke off, her body moving unconsciously in sensuous invitation against his, as though silently speaking the words of love she had just bitten back.

'Say it,' he breathed raggedly, his body tensing as though fighting the invitation of hers, while his hands swept impatiently down the length of her, bringing soft sobs of longing to her lips.

'Love me, Nick,' she sobbed, her mouth open against the silken tautness of his skin, tasting and savouring, while her hands clenched and unclenched against the muscled smoothness of his back, the wildness of the need in her growing beyond endurance.

'That's what I wanted to hear you say,' he whispered, his body stilling hers, tensing for a moment that was like an eternity before it finally took possession of hers.

The sharp cry that escaped her in that fleeting instant of pain was almost drowned by his harsh exclamation of disbelief. But almost before the pain had registered it was negated by an intensity of pleasure welling up and flooding within her; a pleasure so wild and uninhibited, it was imparting itself to him, inflaming him to a fever of abandonment against which he strove for control.

'No,' he groaned softly, perspiration glistening on his body as he tried to impose restraint on himself and on her. 'Sian, what are you doing to me?' he cried out, his teeth sharply punishing against her flesh as wave after wave of exquisite sensation washed through her, till she felt something within her must explode from the sheer surfeit of a pleasure that was almost unbearable. It was then that she sensed the last shreds of control desert him, and it was then that pleasure peaked beyond endurance into a shattering explosion of ecstasy.

Though her gulping lungs ached in their quest to return to a semblance of normality, a dreamlike lethargy was possessing her, and she seemed to drift along on a cloud of bewildered wonderment. And, though the turbulence of her breathing gradually began subsiding, the chaotic turmoil still churning within her warned her that, for her, a return to normality was now an impossibility.

Her eyes lowered to the dark head nestling against her, love filling her with an aching sharpness as she felt the harsh, erratic rhythm of his breathing begin to even out. Then her arms were tightening compulsively as she felt him move, dreading that the moment would come when he would leave her completely.

'Let me ease my weight from you,' he whispered huskily, his arms staying around her, carrying her with him as he moved. 'Sian . . . are you OK?' he asked, his breath a soft whisper against her cheek.

'OK?' she echoed in a daze, clearing her throat at the parched, croaking sound of her own voice. 'How could I possibly be OK?'

'Sian, I just don't understand!' he exclaimed, his words breaking off as his head drew back from her, his eyes searching hers in the ghostly shadows of the moonlight. 'For a moment I thought . . . hell, what does it matter what I thought? There was no way I could have stopped!'

'I'd have killed you if you had,' she informed him mildly, his disjointed, incomprehensible words having not the slightest effect on the dream-like contentment in which she floated.

'What did you say?' he demanded, just as her mouth had begun exploring against his shoulder, savouring the salty tang of his skin.

'Just that I'd——'

'You'd have killed me had I stopped.' He chuckled, laughter rippling through him as he hugged her with a force she felt sure was about to crack her ribs.

A few damaged ribs would be a small price to pay for the happiness now flooding her at his obvious delight, she decided, snuggling contentedly in the fierceness of his hold.

'What I can't understand is why on earth you'd have wanted to . . . stop, I mean.'

'Why on earth, indeed?' he murmured, an answer that was no answer at all.

But there was a gentle possessiveness in his arms as he drew the covers over them and cradled her to him, and it was a gentleness that filled her with a wild surge of hope, echoing, as it seemed to, something akin to the love blazing in every part of her.

He might not be ready for love, she thought dreamily, as his head relaxed with the heaviness of imminent sleep against her breasts, no more than she had been—and a fat lot of difference a lack of readiness had made for her!

CHAPTER TEN

'I'M GLAD everything's all right, but what exactly did Miss Jennings say?' asked Sian, grateful that her tone gave no hint of the apprehension flickering to life inside her. He looked so . . . so normal—how could he possibly look so utterly normal?

She had woken late, astounded that she had even found sleep possible, and more than a little disconcerted to find herself alone, not just in the bed, but in the entire suite. But she hadn't felt, nor even looked, in the least normal. Her mind and body had remained in a confusing, almost erotic state of turmoil as she had bathed and dressed—a turmoil for an instant heightened by Nick's return, but now slowly dissipating into apprehension.

'She was under the impression her housekeeper had explained,' he told her quietly, a wary hesitancy in the eyes that moved across her features.

'Explained what?' asked Sian, the apprehension deepening to a sickening dread as she forced her gaze from the tall, dark-suited figure at the door, everything within her recoiling from what she had glimpsed in those eyes.

'It seems that the day you arrived she'd had a call from Dublin to say a close friend of hers had been involved in an automobile accident. The details had been sketchy, but she was to get more information that evening.' Again those eyes met hers for an instant, and again she felt herself recoil from their message of unease. 'She didn't hear—apparently it was that evening the storms began disrupting the telephone

161

lines. With no means of checking, she spent the night fretting. In the morning she knew she'd have no peace of mind unless she went to Dublin to find out for herself.'

Sian nodded, trying desperately to concentrate on his words as her world silently disintegrated around her. She should have known, she berated herself. Within seconds of her first sight of him standing there—when the memories bombarding her had brought a suffocating joy that made speech impossible—she should have known. When, instead of racing to sweep her into his arms, he had begun speaking of his breakfast meeting with Eithne Jennings, she should have known. But now, the wary disquiet in his eyes had told her with an eloquence far beyond words, and the hurt of that knowledge was a savage wound aching inside her.

'Was her friend badly hurt?' Her words might have sounded strained and detached, but at least she had managed them, she thought bitterly, a terrible need to preserve at least a small shred of dignity flaring in her.

'No—just a broken arm.' As he spoke he began walking towards her, sadness creeping into the eyes that took in her tense pallor.

She stiffened as his hand reached out to stroke her cheek. His pity was the last thing she wanted!

'No, Sian,' he pleaded, as she tried to turn from his touch, his arms suddenly taking her in an embrace that was utterly devoid of passion. 'Whatever you feel, don't feel embarrassment over last night,' he whispered huskily. 'There are times when people need one another—last night was one of those times.'

No, she cried out silently, her rigid body aching to yield to the familiar nearness of his. For him it might have been no more than a purely physical need, yet for her it had been nothing less than an expression of love. And she had been seduced by the uninhibited strength of his passion into believing he had been expressing so much more than just a powerful physical desire. So strong had been her foolish conviction that, in the last of the many times their bodies had fused in a demanding explosion of need, she had been unable to hold back her words of love, crying them out time and again as dawn had broken softly around them.

The passion they had both shared . . . but the only words of love had been hers, she remembered, hot waves of humiliation wafting over her as she tried to pull free from the arms that now withheld even passion.

'We'd best get some breakfast into you,' he told her gently, as she broke free. 'I've ordered a cab to take us to the airport—it'll be here in less than an hour.'

'I'm not hungry,' she muttered, turning from him and picking up her handbag from the sofa. 'I'd better get my things together,' she added, rummaging through her handbag as though there were a purpose to her actions—her only purpose being to allow her aching lungs to fill with the air so suddenly torn from them. He hadn't been able to wait to escape this place, with its memories of his moment of weakness. She gave a small cry as she felt his hands on her shoulders.

'Sian, there's a reason for all this haste,' he said quietly.

She froze, a silent, pleading cry tearing through her as she willed him not to put into words what she already had understood.

'I also had a call from Margaret this morning. It seems Simon Porter is defying all medical statistics—his speech has returned and a good deal of his mobility. So we——'

The rest of his words were lost to her ears as she turned

and leaned against him, silent sobs racking her body.

'Hey, that was meant to be good news,' he chided softly, his arms enfolding her as she tried to ignore the small voice inside her which was chiding her for the hypocrisy of the tears that had little to do with Simon.

In the days that came, even that small voice of conscience deserted her, leaving her alone with the bleak, despairing void that had gradually replaced her capacity for thought—thoughts brought only pain.

'I'm sorry I couldn't make it for lunch,' she apologised to Anna, as they made their way into her office.

'Not to worry, Toby wanted——' Anna broke off, her eyes widening in alarm for an instant before she was able to bring them under control. 'It seems the wanderer's returned,' she quipped, attempting to inject humour into her tone, as her eyes rose anxiously from the light glowing on the telephone console to Sian's pale and noticeably tense face.

With a listless shrug, Sian drew out her chair and sat down. She was frantically racking her brains for something to say—just a few witty, unconcerned words—anything to help mask the devastation being wrought within her. She had noticed the tell-tale light a split second before Anna, and had only just managed to get her chair from under her desk before her legs had buckled completely beneath her.

'So he has,' she managed at last, her reawakened thoughts hurtling back over the past three days.

A brittle brightness had sustained her during the taxi ride from the village. She had talked practically non-stop of Simon and how much she owed him professionally. But all the while she had been conscious of Nick's concern, mentally shrinking from the pity behind that concern even as she shrank from her own words echoing like accusations in her mind; those words of love torn from her as she had lain in the enchantment of his arms; words echoing within her like humiliating taunts, till her only escape was to block every vestige of thought from her tormented mind.

He had immediately sensed the barriers she had begun erecting so painstakingly, and it was the uncharacteristically cautious hesitancy of his words, as he tried several times to penetrate those barriers, that only added to her conviction that to him their night of passion was a momentary weakness he had instantly regretted.

He had tried again when they had eventually returned to the office.

'Sian, I don't want to see you like this. Have dinner with me this evening . . . perhaps talking might help.'

There had been such gentleness in his words—such sadness in his eyes, she remembered. But his impatience had quickly flared in the face of the impenetrable barriers cloaking her in their protection. That he had been nowhere near the office in the two days since that final fruitless confrontation, she had welcomed with a strangely childlike gratitude, refusing even to contemplate his inevitable return.

'At least I'm just about over the after-effects of that bug I seemed to have picked up in Ireland,' she murmured diffidently, wondering what on earth had possessed her to refer to that spur-of-the-moment story invented in the face of Anna and Toby's shocked concern on her return . . . a story which had fooled neither of them for even a moment, she thought dejectedly, spotting the flash of scepticism in her friend's look before it was quickly brought under control.

Tonight she would talk to Anna. Her panic-stricken reaction to Nick's return was a warning of just how close to breaking-point she was—even confiding in someone as loving as Anna would be a humiliating experience, but for her sanity's sake it was something she would have to do. As though in confirmation of her thoughts, she reached out and caught Anna's hand.

'Tonight,' she began, shocked to hear the hoarse fear in her voice, 'there's something I . . .' She jumped visibly as the door of Nick's office flew open.

'Sian—I need to speak to you. Now!' Then he disappeared, leaving the door still open.

'Good luck,' whispered Anna, leaning over and giving her shoulder a reassuring squeeze.

Unable to bring herself to meet her friend's eyes, Sian rose, resolutely blanking her mind once more as she entered the office and closed the door behind her.

Her almost violent physical reaction to the sight of that lean, athletic frame, sprawled carelessly in the large swivel-chair, horrified her. It was as though he had become a drug for which her addicted body now shamelessly craved.

'Did you go to see Simon?' he asked abruptly.

'No . . . not yet,' she stammered, confused by the unexpectedness of that abrupt question. Simon knew her too well not to recognise the change in her; she had been unable to face his inevitable cross-examination as to the reason. 'I thought I'd wait till——'

'As expected, he's cleared up the Henderson mystery,' he cut in tonelessly. 'I didn't want him bothered with the affair, but it seems he handed Alan Hunter all the relevant papers today. Sian, do you have any idea what a fool I've been making of myself, thanks to this neat little blend of fact and fancy of yours?' His face as expressionless as the tone of his voice, he lifted the two files before him, holding them aloft before letting them drop back to his desk with a dull thud. 'Come here!'

Scarcely aware that she was doing so, she obeyed his harsh command, blanching visibly in the moment she reached his desk and recognised the files lying on it.

'Without your deliberate sabotage, I'd have nailed Henderson and his phoney threats weeks ago,' he continued in a chillingly quiet voice. 'As it was, I was tying myself in knots, arguing at cross purposes with nearly every protagonist, because I foolishly assumed I was in possession of *facts*.'

'Nick, it wasn't deliberate sabotage——'

'Oh, no?' His face pale with fury, he flung open one of the files, his forefinger stabbing angrily at a carbon copy of a letter bearing her name as the sender. 'Let's take this particular piece of fiction! This had me convinced the guy concerned was in league with Henderson. What the hell else could I think when he denied all knowledge of it?'

'That's one of the very few I felt it necessary to alter substantially,' croaked Sian, unable to believe what was happening to her—the whole subject had gone clean out of her mind.

'Hell, I don't believe I'm hearing this . . . one of the very few you felt it necessary to alter substantially? Well, I have news for you—this just happens to be one of the few that gave me every appearance of being an out and out nutcase! I guess the others—the ones you only felt it necessary to alter minimally—merely left me looking an incompetent fool! These people must have got it into their heads I was too dumb to think of reading our own file copies! Can you blame them?'

'Nick, I'm sorry it's all backfired on you——'

'But why, Sian? Why did you do it?' he asked hoarsely.

'Because . . . because I thought I could protect Simon. I . . .'

'And who was it you were so busy trying to protect Simon from?' he demanded icily.

'From you,' she blurted out, flinching at the bleak coldness in his eyes. 'I thought you'd fire him——'

'You thought I'd fire him?' he echoed, his tone suddenly weary.

'Nick, I . . .' She wanted to tell him that had been a long time ago—that she *would* have told him but for Margaret expressly forbidding her to do so, but it was pointless dragging Margaret into this now, she decided miserably, her eyes rising to plead with his, then flinching from what they found. 'Nick——'

'Sian, please . . . just leave,' he muttered hoarsely, leaning back in his chair and closing his eyes.

She hesitated, trying to control the violent trembling that had begun racking her entire body.

'The way I feel, right at this moment . . .' His oddly dazed words faltered. 'Please . . . just leave.'

She turned and slowly walked from him. His justifiable anger she could take—the relative quietness of that anger only seemed to stress its depth—but what left her trembling and feeling physically sick was the stark hatred she had witnessed in his eyes; a hatred every bit as powerful as the love that ached incessantly in her night and day, a joyless love that was destroying her, like a sickness that knew no cure.

* * *

Sian screwed up the sheet of paper on which she had begun her seventh attempt at a letter of resignation, and hurled it despondently in the general direction of the waste-paper basket—missing, as had the majority of her other aims.

With an exclamation of impatience, she flung down her pen and glanced at her watch—it was almost seven and still no sign of either Toby or Anna. She frowned, anxiety creeping across features still bearing the tell-tale ravages of an earlier bout of exhausting weeping. Where on earth were they? She remembered Toby's promise to pick them up from work, but nothing of any plans he and Anna had for this evening. Then she remembered Anna's earlier call. The phone had began ringing as she had entered the flat, her mind still reeling from having stormed from the office with the intention of never again returning. Anna's anxious words of concern had suddenly faltered and their conversation had ended abruptly. Intuition had instantly informed her what had happened, bringing her a vivid, mental image of Nick lounging at the door of Anna's office. It was when other images of him began filling her mind, refusing her any means of escape from the savage pain of their persistence, that she had disintegrated into the mindless bout of weeping that had left her listless and exhausted.

Appalled to find her eyes filling once more, she made a concentrated effort to steer her mind from its dangerous train of thought. Perhaps Anna had intended telling her that she and Toby had something planned for this evening—though it was puzzling that Anna hadn't even returned home to change . . .

She started as she heard a key in the door, rising as she heard the faint murmur of voices, and slumping back in her seat as the softness of a familiar American accent seemed to reach her.

She was going clean out of her mind, she informed herself savagely, as her straining ears now picked up nothing other than the vague sounds of someone in the hall, followed by Toby's familiar voice calling her name.

'I'm in the study,' she called, clenching her hands into fists in an attempt to control their sudden shaking. Hearing voices was a pretty strong indication it was about time she started pulling herself together, she informed herself sharply, turning as she heard Toby enter.

'What are you doing closeted in here?' he asked, strolling towards the writing bureau, gazing down at her, with unfamiliar speculation in his eyes.

'Writing my letter of resignation,' replied Sian, thrown slightly by the lack of sympathy in his look, though she had no doubt Anna would have told him of her spectacular walk out. 'Where's Anna—and why are you both so late?'

'Anna's decided to wait at my place,' he replied unhelpfully, other considerations obviously on his mind. 'Sian, I believe you ran into Jimmy Smithers at Sir George Linton's place.'

'Yes, didn't I mention it?' she asked, completely thrown by the unexpectedness of his words, and experiencing a childish surge of indignation that he could be so unfeeling —he must know she would be pretty upset; it wasn't every day she walked out of her job. At the best of times, Jimmy Smithers was hardly the most scintillating of topics of conversation.

'No, you didn't. What did he say?' he asked, annoying her by fiddling with the neatly stacked pile of stationery on her desk.

'I can't honestly remember,' she snapped, pushing his hand away from the paper. 'He probably sent you his regards—I'm sorry I forgot to give you them, they obviously mean so much to you!'

'Surely you can remember something of what he said?' persisted Toby blandly, seemingly oblivious of her tone.

'No, I can't!' she retorted heatedly, thoroughly disgruntled by his unfeeling attitude. Surely he must realise the last thing she needed was this cross-examination? 'It was just as Jimmy spotted me that Mike Grade arrived with the news about Sir George. Toby, is there by any remote chance a point to all this?' she added sharply. Surely this couldn't be his idea of distracting her from her problems, she thought disbelievingly, then immediately dismissed the idea.

'There is. You can't remember *anything* Jimmy said before the interruption?'

'For heaven's sake, Toby, I've told you!' she groaned in angry frustration. 'His conversation is hardly memorable —you know what Jimmy's like.'

'Oh, yes,' murmured Toby, flashing her a look she found impossible to interpret. 'You and I know only too well what Jimmy is like—the trouble is, there are a lot of others who don't.'

'And what exactly is that supposed to mean?' demanded Sian, rising to her feet in complete exasperation. There were times when she had known Toby deliberately pick a fight, times when his tendency to get a bee in his bonnet over something, to the exclusion of all else, would drive her to fury—but she had never known him behave quite as perplexingly as he was now. Her eyes widened in alarm as a sudden thought occurred to her.

'Toby, have you had a row with Anna?' she asked, convinced she had hit on the reason for this most peculiar behaviour, and mentally kicking herself for her lack of understanding.

'No, I haven't had a row with Anna,' he replied, with a grin she found particularly infuriating. 'Though, to be truthful, I had to exercise a great deal of self-control when I arrived to collect the pair of you and found her metaphorically holding your soon-to-be-erstwhile boss's hand.'

'She was what?' croaked Sian, flopping back weakly on the chair.

'Being the open-minded, understanding type, I took the pair of them off for a drink,' Toby went on.

Sian's mouth opened, but words refused to come out. Not only was she completely confused, she was also stunned by what she could only see as his treachery.

Shaking his head in gentle rebuke, Toby pulled her to her feet. 'Stop looking at me as though I were some sort of Judas,' he admonished, hugging her. 'This evening I discovered that Nick Sinclair is the sort of man I have a lot of time for.'

In silence, Sian hugged him back. Her reaction was irrational—Toby had no idea what was going on inside her, and, even if he had, it was illogical of her to expect him to dislike Nick.

'There are times, McAllister, when I almost despair of you,' he teased gently. 'Heaven knows, I've tried to do my brotherly best by you; tried to educate you to understand the mysteries that constitute we men.'

'You failed miserably because you're a crummy example —you're too nice,' choked Sian, through tears and laughter. 'So I suppose it won't come as much of a surprise to you to hear that my latest encounter with the mysteries of one of your lot has been as disastrous as all the others.

'Poor little Sian,' he sighed, releasing her and gazing

sadly down at her. 'I take it we're referring to one Nicholas Sinclair?'

Miserably, she nodded. 'But I don't feel up to talking about it just yet.' That she had opened up even this much surprised her.

'That's the trouble with you,' he remarked, his tone suddenly curt as he moved towards the door. 'You don't talk—but there are times when even the apparently obvious needs talking about.'

'You know that, apart from you, I've always had difficulty confiding in people,' she exclaimed defensively. 'Anyway, I was going to talk to Anna this evening.'

'What the hell good will talking to Anna do you?' he snapped. 'For Pete's sake, Sian, the person you should be talking to is Nick!'

'I don't want to talk to him, I——'

'Tough, because he wants to speak to you,' interrupted Toby, with undisguised impatience. 'And it would pay you to listen to him, if only to stop you gratuitously resigning from a job you both need and enjoy.'

Hurt by the harshness of his words, Sian tried to explain. 'Toby, you don't understand—I *couldn't* work with him,' she whispered dejectedly.

'The point is, you wouldn't have to. He's had enough— he's jacking the whole thing in and going back to New York!'

By the time she had absorbed the impact of those words, he had gone.

'Toby!' she cried, racing after him and reaching the hall only in time to see the front door close behind him.

She leaned her head against the cool wood of the door, a feeling of utter desolation seeping through her. It was the best thing that could happen to her, she reasoned—

a thought that only strengthened her terrible sense of desolation. It could only be easier to bear, knowing he was no longer in the same city—the same country—as she. Once he had felt the need to put an ocean between himself and the woman he had loved, and now she fully understood the terrible compulsion behind that need. She stiffened, a sickening dread now mingling with her desolation. Patty! Patty, who had crossed the ocean he had placed between them. And now he was returning—to Patty? Perhaps even with her.

She jumped back from the door, startled by its soft chimes pealing in her ears.

'Toby, I'm sorry,' she was protesting as she dragged open the door. 'I didn't mean to . . .' Her agitated words trailed to silence, her expression freezing to one of horror as she found herself face to face with Nick.

For several seconds they faced one another, silent combatants assessing the opposition until the moment the tall American gave a barely perceptible shrug, then strolled past her and into the hall.

'You didn't seem about to invite me in—so I've invited myself,' he stated, the cool eyes subjecting her to their impersonal examination, bringing it forcefully home to her just how drab and dishevelled she must look. 'You may as well close the door,' he informed her brusquely. 'What I have to say could take some time.'

Stifling the immediate anger she felt at his autocratic tone, Sian let the door swing closed. While he was here she was going to show nothing but dignity, she vowed, even if she dropped down dead from the strain once he had gone!

'The living-room's in here,' she stated with cool politeness, walking past him without betraying so much as a flicker of the devastating turmoil churning within her. 'Would you like me to take your coat?' she asked, as he shrugged it off. Ignoring his scowling silence, and the coat which he immediately flung across the armchair furthest from him, she tried another tack. 'Perhaps you'd like a coffee?'

'I had one next door,' he snapped, his eyes narrowing in their unremitting scrutiny of her, as he threw himself on to the nearer of the two armchairs, his long legs stretched out before him.

'So—what was it you wished to say?' asked Sian, in a bright, hostessy voice she knew was just about guaranteed to rile him.

His retaliation was swift, coming just as she had primly seated herelf on the sofa opposite him.

'You look a mess,' he stated, with no attempt at disguising the obvious satisfaction he derived from the observation.

Tensing with fury, Sian tried to calm herself by counting—she reached five. 'And you are a boor!' Damn it, she cursed silently, seething with a rage she found almost impossible to control—she should have counted to ten—twenty. 'And don't try consoling yourself that's my reaction to American males in general—its my exclusive opinion of you!'

'This American male doesn't need to look far for any consolation he might need—this is the one in whose arms you spent a night, telling him how much you loved him—remember?' he drawled softly.

Sian felt the colour drain from her face. She *was* out of her mind! She actually loved a man who could stoop this low! If there had been anything within arm's reach, she knew she would have picked it up and hurled it at him the instant he had uttered those taunting words.

'People say the most ludicrous things in the heat of the moment—that you even remember them tells me you're an even bigger fool than I'd judged you,' she managed, surprised she hadn't actually screamed the words at him.

'You think I'm a fool, do you?' he demanded, his voice ominously quiet.

It was the sight of the small muscle beating a warning tattoo at his cheek that checked Sian's furious retort. He was about to explode, she warned herself, and then his words so far would be mild in comparison to the rapier cruelty of those he would undoubtedly let fly. Suddenly she felt utterly drained, both physically and emotionally.

'No, Nick, I don't think you're a fool. And no matter what you think—even though you've always refused to admit it—I've never harboured any feelings that are even remotely anti-American.'

'Funnily enough, I've never believed you have—though sometimes my belief seemed more like an act of faith,' he stated wryly. 'How come you, and only you, out of all the staff, remained so certain I'd show no sympathy towards Simon Porter?'

'If you're referring to those wretched files, I was merely trying to hedge every bet there was in Simon's favour. As things stood, you'd have been entirely within your rights to fire him,' she protested, almost wincing at the garbled sound of her inadequate explanation.

'A point the others no longer saw as a possibility once they'd got to know me,' he stated quietly. 'Yet you altered those files long after you'd had a chance to form an opinion of me—which doesn't say much for the opinion you finally formed.'

Sian glanced up, thrown by what almost sounded like

regret in his tone—his face was completely without expression.

'Nick, I wish you wouldn't see it like that. The only thing it reflected was my deep regard for Simon . . . I still find it difficult to admit I could have behaved so stupidly, so completely irresponsibly . . . I never once stopped to think out the possible consequences of my actions. I never for one moment dreamed you'd actually check the correspondence . . .'

'You thought I'd skim through the files and decide that if anyone was to be fired it was you?'

'If it came to that—yes. But more than anything I was banking on something coming up to vindicate Simon.'

'Had it come to it, I'd have had to fire you both,' he pointed out, the hint of amusement in his tone startling her. 'After you left this afternoon, Margaret explained that she'd forbidden you to tell me about the alterations, but as my assistant, your duty was to me, not to her. There again, I guess it would have been asking for too great a step out of character—expecting you to tell me anything.'

There was puzzlement on Sian's face as her gaze met the cool enigmatic blue of his.

'You've always made a point of telling me as little as you possibly can,' he stated expressionlessly.

She had told him she loved him, for heaven's sake, she cried out silently.

'Nick, I honestly don't know what you mean,' she whispered hoarsely. These moments were the worst she had ever experienced—ones she should be praying to have behind her as quickly as possible—yet a part of her wanted them to drag out into eternity, because once they were gone she knew he would be gone forever with them.

'The day I interviewed you,' he stated abruptly. 'I admit

I made some pretty mean remarks about your privileged background. But how come it was only today that I learned, from Anna, how much you needed your job, how drastically your circumstances have altered?'

'But you were a complete stranger then! I could hardly have——'

'For how long did I stay a stranger?' he countered angrily. 'Was I still a stranger the night of Linton's ball? I guess I must have been, because you made no attempt then to explain to me that the guy you were living with—the guy who you had doing his share of the cooking—was not the live-in lover it then seemed perfectly reasonable for me to believe he was!'

'Jimmy Smithers!' she groaned in weak disbelief, trying desperately to recall Toby's earlier, incomprehensible words. 'This is ridiculous—you can't possibly have thought Toby and I were lovers!' she exclaimed, aghast, suddenly tossing aside her scrutiny of her cousin's words as Nick's finally sank in. 'He's my cousin. He's like a brother . . . how could you possibly——?'

'How could I possibly? he interrupted coldly. 'If some guy literally waltzes up to you and says "I hear you and so-and-so are living at such-and-such a place and that you've got him doing the cooking,' what the hell am I supposed to think?' He leapt to his feet, his face dark with anger as he rammed his hands in his pockets and began pacing back and forth in front of the sofa on which Sian sat rigid with disbelief.

'Can't you understand that Jimmy's words just didn't register with me?' she pleaded. 'Mike was trying to attract my attention . . . to tell us about Sir George.'

'OK, but how about the tears in Ireland when you heard of the engagement?' he intoned, coming to a sudden halt before her. 'And don't tell me they were tears of joy—I know you too well to swallow that one!'

'They weren't for joy.' The harsh catch in her voice warned her she was on the verge of tears—a humiliation from which she felt certain she would never recover should they materialise. 'Before he told me about himself and Anna, Toby had broken the news to me that my dog had died. Pathetic, isn't it?' she rounded on him in a fury that was directed more at herself as she felt the dreaded tears break free. 'Perhaps he *was* only an animal, but I happened to love him!'

'Hey, Sian, take it easy,' he began softly, dropping to his haunches before her, his eyes wary. 'No matter how crazy I sound, I have to have my say, I have to get things straight——'

'Why should I take things easy?' she shrieked, cutting through his words, uncaring of how big a fool she was making of herself as something finally snapped in her. 'I want *my* say! Go back to New York, where you belong—to your damned Patty! You deserve one another!'

'Patty means nothing to me—I didn't even meet with her when she was over. Here,' he added brusquely, rising as he handed her a large, white handkerchief. 'You look an even worse mess now.'

'I hate you!' she seethed, that final insult blotting out his other words as she angrily scrubbed her cheeks. The handkerchief she then hurled at his retreating back floated weightlessly to her feet. At least the mortifying flood of tears had stopped, she consoled herself, glowering as he turned once more to face her.

'Sian, hasn't the significance of anything I've been saying got through to you?' he asked quietly.

He looked so pale, she thought, furious with herself for

the sharp stab of anxiety automatically accompanying the thought.

'You thought I was having some sort of incestuous relationship with——'

'Quit acting so dumb!' he exclaimed impatiently. 'A relationship between cousins can't be termed incestuous —not that you made any attempt to explain the guy was your cousin——'

'Why should I feel the need to explain anything to you?' she retorted defensively. 'From the day you arrived you did nothing but snarl at me!'

'Only because you got under my skin—right from that first day.'

There was something in his tone, something other than its sudden lack of anger, that made her glance up in puzzlement.

'Why you should saddle me with an imaginary lover— just because you found me irritating——'

'I said you got under my skin,' he interrupted icily. 'And even you must agree, the way that guy spoke at Linton's it wouldn't have taken an overly fertile imagination to think you had a lover.'

'I've already told you . . . I wasn't paying any attention to what Jimmy was saying,' she protested.

'Sian, I asked you if the significance of what I've been saying has got through to you,' he repeated, ignoring her protest. 'Why didn't you tell me about your dog?'

'How am I supposed to answer any of your questions when you keep adding more?' she burst out angrily. 'I'm not one of your wretched criminals in a witness-box, so stop subjecting me to this third degree! I didn't tell you about my dog because . . . because of the mood you were in. I couldn't have faced your sarcastic remarks . . . so I just didn't tell you,' she finished wearily.

'You thought I'd make sarcastic remarks,' he sighed. 'And I, convinced you had a lover, thought you were in tears because you'd just heard you'd lost him to Anna.' His eyes met hers, tentative, uncertain eyes; then the ghost of a smile curved his mouth. 'It's like the plot of some third-rate farce. Is it any wonder I'm incapable of thinking straight?'

'Except that in farces nothing gets unravelled until the very last scene, whereas you learned that night I'd never had a lover,' she told him, her words softly bitter as they expressed what had only then dawned on her.

'They say that the real test of love is whether or not you can put the loved one before all considerations of yourself,' he stated expressionlessly. 'That night I was prepared to do anything to ease the pain I was convinced you were suffering . . . to be second best for you, if that was what you needed.'

'Nick!' It was the hollow chill of his words that sent a shiver running through her, bringing his name to her lips in a soft cry of protest.

'You're right,' he continued, his eyes hooded from her sight as he trained them downwards. 'I knew I was the first . . . for one incredible moment I . . . there are no words to describe how I felt in that moment. I had to keep telling myself there was someone you loved—someone you had lived with, even though you and he were never lovers. I couldn't for the life of me fathom out why that should have been so—all I knew was that there was this other guy, and that for some crazy reason I was your first lover merely by default.'

As those soft, chillingly toneless words poured from him, Sian rose. She walked towards him, her footsteps slow and uncertain as she waited in dread for the meaning in those words to alter. Their meaning remained unchanged as she reached him, to rest first her hands against his chest, then her cheek against the slow, angry thud of his heart.

'I told you how I loved you,' she whispered protestingly, pressing closer to his tense, unyielding body. 'I told you, yet you said nothing.'

She gave a sharp gasp of pain as his fingers sank into her hair, dragging her head back till she was looking up into the grim set of his face.

'Ironic, isn't it?' He gave a bitter, humourless laugh. 'What you felt so free to say, in the heat of the moment—as you put it—I was unable to say . . . yet I'd have been the one speaking the truth.'

She had difficulty unravelling his words, feeling uncertain and untrusting of the fluttering sensation trying to break free within her. Had she ever allowed herself to dream of hearing his words of love, she knew they would have been words that danced in delight around her ears, not these grim, passionless words that seemed almost a contradiction of love.

'Nick,' she whispered, that fluttering promise of happiness gaining hold in her, as she steeled herself against the tone of his words and concentrated solely on their meaning, 'what's happened to that sharp lawyer's mind of yours? How could you possibly believe any woman could live with a man she loved and remain a virgin? And whatever your thoughts about Toby and me when we were in Ireland, today you've learned the truth——' She broke off as she felt a sudden shiver ripple through him.

'I told you—I can't think straight any more,' he protested hoarsely, his arms slipping around her to hold her in a curiously weightless embrace.

'Nick, there was no one for you to be consoling me over

. . . for me there could be only one reason for taking a lover, and I told you that reason . . . yet the next morning, you were so distant, so . . .'

'No!' he protested hoarsely, his arms tightening fiercely. 'I was silently begging you for just one sign. Sian, I needed your words of love in the cool light of morning, because I couldn't allow myself to trust what you had said so freely in passion.'

She buried her face against him, words of protest tumbling from her. 'If you'd known how I felt, you'd have known how false your reasoning had been—no man on this earth could ever have brought me a shred of consolation for not having your love!'

Her head was lifted by gentle, guiding hands.

'It's always been yours for the taking,' he murmured huskily, his mouth seeking hers. 'Oh, Sian,' he groaned, his lips parting hers in a restless, searching kiss, 'what can I do but plead insanity? The only remotely sane thing I've done in weeks, I did this afternoon, when I went to Anna and asked her to explain your relationship with Toby.' As he spoke he was placing soft, frantic kisses all around her mouth. 'By the time I'd heard her out, my mind had taken off on a trip of its own—I guess it's still out there somewhere, celebrating its escape from a fool.'

'No,' she protested fiercely, her lips nuzzling in softness against his, trying to impart their comfort.

'Oh, yes,' he murmured softly. 'Only a fool would have fought as I did—fighting what was happening to me—denying what had probably begun happening to me the day I interviewed you . . . the day all those crazy sparks started hitting the air.'

'That soon?' she murmured, a shiver of pure happiness jolting through her.

'That soon,' he confirmed with a softly rumbling chuckle. 'I didn't know I had it in me to be such a heel—letting you believe that what I'd overheard you dishing out to Lloyd had a bearing on my behaviour.' He drew back slightly from her, his eyes filled with a blatant message of love as they gazed down into hers. 'Sian, I love you. It's a relief to be able to say it . . . I love you . . . I . . .'

'Am I not to be allowed to get a word in edgeways?' she demanded softly, unable to distinguish between the love and happiness brimming over inside her, then coming to the conclusion that they were indistinguishable. There was a trembling uncertainty in her fingers as they reached up and began tracing the outline of his mouth. 'I only wanted to tell you how much I love you . . .'

'Only?' he teased softly.

'But first of all I have to check if you're real . . . ouch!' she yelped, as his teeth caught and firmly nipped one of her fingers.

'I'm real all right.'

'Are you? You'll probably have to draw blood—a pint at least—before I even begin to feel certain,' she whispered, the ghosts of remembered pain sending a sudden shiver coursing through her.

His arms tightened protectively. 'I have a better idea—though I'll gladly chomp away at your fingers all you like if my idea doesn't appeal.'

'As long as it doesn't involve sticking pins in me,' she murmured, the dark memories receding as her cheek nestled against the quickening throb of his heart.

'Did you just read my mind?' he demanded through soft laughter. 'Because that's what it will involve, if we do it in the States—and, of course, only if you agree.'

'I think I'll settle for the odd bite or two,' she murmured

contentedly.

'So, you're turning down my proposal of marriage even before I've had a chance to get the words out—is that it?'

She tried to pull free, struggling against the hand that held her head firmly against him, in her desperate need to look into his face.

'What's that got to do with having pins stuck in me?' she asked, giving up the unequal struggle as her breath seemed to swell into a constricting pain in her chest.

'Not pins, exactly. But we'll need blood tests if we marry in the States,' he explained, with exaggerated patience.

'Oh.' She was trying desperately to speak, but the words were just refusing to come.

'Sian—"oh" yes, or "oh" no? Plain "oh" just leaves me strung out with suspense.'

Not only was she incapable of speech, at this the most deliriously happy moment of her life, but she was suddenly being racked by gulping sobs over which she had absolutely no control.

'It's all right, my darling,' he soothed, lifting her in his arms. He carried her to the sofa, cradling her against him as he sat down. 'Sian, believe me, I understand. I've had a few hours' headstart on you and my mind's still a crazy jumble.'

'I just don't believe this is happening!' she sobbed in protest. 'How can I expect you to believe this is the happiest moment of my life, with me carrying on like this? You could take me to Outer Mongolia and stick a thousand pins in me and I wouldn't care! I'd still want to marry you!'

'Boston or London will do,' he murmured with a softly indulgent chuckle.

'Boston, of course!' she stated promptly.

'Why so positively Boston?' he asked, still laughing.

'Because your father doesn't like flying.'

'Because my father doesn't like flying.' He repeated the words softly, as though turning them over in his mind and examining each one minutely. Then he stooped and retrieved the handkerchief she had earlier thrown at him and began gently drying her tears. 'This scrap of cotton is certainly earning its keep,' he muttered gruffly. Then suddenly he was hugging her fiercely to him. 'Oh, Sian, have you any idea how I love you?' he whispered passionately. 'It frightens me even thinking of how I've behaved towards you; how I could so easily have driven you away; always showing you my bad side—a side far worse than I'd known I possessed!'

'Yet all it took was one glimpse of the good side and no other man existed as far as I was concerned,' she murmured consolingly, unable to remember a time when her heart had not been fully occupied with loving him.

'Just the merest glimpse?' he queried, his lips, now exploring softly against her throat, sending shivers of excitement rippling through her.

'Just the merest glimpse,' she confirmed, her arms creeping up round his neck. 'When Anna and Toby . . .' She gave a soft cry of protest as he heaved himself free of her arms.

'Hell!' he groaned, and began laughing weakly. 'Anna and Toby, they . . .'

'What exactly did you three say to one another?' demanded Sian, shaking him as he slumped heavily against her, still laughing. 'Nick?' she pleaded, trying unsuccessfully to fight off the infection of his laughter. 'I couldn't understand why Toby seemed to have a bee in his bonnet about Jimmy Smithers when he came in. Nick, exactly what *was* said?' she exclaimed through her own chuckles, sinking her fingers into his hair and attempting to drag his head up from her.

'Don't ask,' he pleaded weakly. 'All I know is the pair of them kept looking at me as though I were some sort of a moron!'

'This I have to hear!' Sian giggled, giving a yelp of protest as he suddenly leapt to his feet, lifting her with him.

'How about showing the man you're going to marry some of that loving concern you displayed towards his pa?' he demanded, his eyes darkening noticeably as he caught her to him.

'I couldn't bear the thought of him having to fly here for . . . You're trying to change the subject!' she accused indignantly, then promptly rose on her tiptoes and lifted her lips invitingly to his.

'Oh, no, you don't,' he protested half-heartedly, before visibly bracing himself to grasp her by the shoulders and hold her away from him. 'One of the reasons, my irresistible little seductress, that we're getting out of here pronto, is the shameless way you're taxing my will-power!'

'Irresistible, my foot,' she murmured contentedly. 'The way your will-power is dealing with my shamelessness isn't doing much for my self-confidence, I can tell you.'

His answer was to frogmarch her into the hall. It was only when he had the front door open that he relented, sweeping her into a fierce bear-hug. 'Wow—I never thought I'd make it out of there with my virtue intact!' His voice grew husky as he rubbed his cheek against hers. 'And as for your self-confidence, we have the rest of our lives for me to set about doing a repair job on that.'

'It's just made a miraculous recovery,' she murmured, terrified that she was about to burst into tears once more from the sheer excess of happiness with which his teasing words had filled her.

He slipped his arm around her, closing the front door behind them. 'I feel safer with that closed,' he grinned down at her. 'Because my will-power really is at rock bottom.'

'So why are we going next door?' she murmured unhelpfully. 'I take it we *are* on our way to Toby's flat?'

He nodded, steering her purposefully along the hallway. 'I always do right by my friends . . .'

'Friends?' teased Sian, feeling almost giddy with happiness. 'So you didn't take offence—at them regarding you as a moron?'

He threw back his head and laughed. 'How else could they regard me? Friends—definitely,' He halted, his face suddenly serious as he gazed down at her. 'Sian, loving you was destroying me—I'd reached a point where my mind couldn't tell up from down. Right up until a few moments ago, I was incapable of recognising just what those two were doing for me—for us. When Anna shoved me through that door and out into this corridor, with instructions to get on with saying whatever needed saying to you——'

'Anna actually did that?' choked Sian, her emotions hovering bizarrely between anguish and weak laughter.

'Hell, I hope you're not going to prove as callous as she has!' he exclaimed indignantly, resuming his energetic stride. 'The only reason I came to you was that I was rendered even more dazed and confused by the brutality of her treatment. And stop giggling!' he admonished as they reached the door, with her collapsed weakly against him. 'Toby was saying something about booking a table somewhere, for four, as I was ejected——Pull yourself together,' he protested, grinning down at her. 'I remember thinking—dazed and confused though I was—that they would be the only two eating . . .'

'Nicholas Sinclair, are you telling me this dash round here is because you're thinking about your stomach?' asked Sian in mock indignation.

'You have to understand—I haven't eaten for days, the state I've been in over you. But no,' he continued, his expression suddenly pious. 'Your cousin's final words were that I should get on with it, as he and Anna would be holding their breath.' He was now grinning wickedly. 'And just in case he's in need of mouth-to-mouth resuscitation— I'll be the one giving it. You're not the only one around here still not one hundred per cent sure all this can be real.'

Just to make certain of reality, he took her into his arms, and it was some considerable time before they both felt sufficiently reassured—enough, that was, to get round to ringing the doorbell.

Coming Next Month

#1295 ONE MORE NIGHT Lindsay Armstrong
Evonne expected to be helping a young untried writer to organize and finish his book. It was a favor to her employer. Instead, Rick Emerson was a sophisticated, attractive, dangerous specimen who constantly disturbed her....

#1296 MY DESTINY Rosemary Hammond
When detective Stephen Ryan made it clear he wanted to see more of her, Joanna remembered the last man she'd loved. Three years ago she'd been married to Ross, also a policeman, and he'd died in the line of duty. Couldn't the same thing happen to Stephen?

#1297 FREE SPIRIT Penny Jordan
Hannah Maitland knew exactly what she wanted out of life, and men didn't rate very high on her list. She'd never been tempted away from her chosen path... until she went to work for Silas Jeffreys.

#1298 A MOST UNSUITABLE WIFE Roberta Leigh
Her modeling career hadn't prepared her for child caring—but Lorraine was determined to care for her brother's children, orphaned by an accident. It wasn't easy—and her arrogant, authoritarian neighbor Jason Fletcher only added to her problems....

#1299 LOVE IS FOR THE LUCKY Susanne McCarthy
Ros had learned her lesson about men long ago and now kept her emotions firmly controlled. Then Jordan Griffin came on the scene tempting her to weaken—though she couldn't see why a famous rock star would be interested in her.

#1300 RENDEZVOUS IN RIO Elizabeth Oldfield
Christa had been forced to leave Jefferson Barssi because of his arrogance and hard-heartedness. She and their son had been away from Brazil for six months. Now she was forced to return—and Jefferson didn't seem to have changed at all!

#1301 STEEL TIGER Kay Thorpe
Jan thought that Don Felipe de Rimados wanted a secretary. Actually he wanted a son! She was attracted to him, but could she possibly comply with her unusual contract of employment—only to walk away afterward?

#1302 THREAT OF POSSESSION Sara Wood
Roxy Page was stunned when she inherited Carnock—after all, she was only the housekeeper's daughter. Ethan Tremaine would go to any lengths to have the house back in the family, so she knew she'd have to be on guard against him....

Available in September wherever paperback books are sold, or through Harlequin Reader Service:

In the U.S.
901 Fuhrmann Blvd.
P.O. Box 1397
Buffalo, N.Y. 14240-1397

In Canada
P.O. Box 603
Fort Erie, Ontario
L2A 5X3

COMING SOON...

For years Harlequin and Silhouette novels have been taking readers places—but only in their imaginations.

This fall look for PASSPORT TO ROMANCE, a promotion that could take you around the corner or around the world!

Watch for it in September!

★